C000120687

THE BLACK MARBLE POOL

BY STAN LEVENTHAL

AMETHYST PRESS

NEW YORK, NY

This book is a work of fiction. Any similarity between persons, places, and things in this text and actual persons (living or dead), places, and things, is purely coincidental.

AN AMETHYST PRESS FIRST EDITION
COPYRIGHT © 1990 by STAN LEVENTHAL

Published in the United States of America by Amethyst Press, Inc., 462 Broadway, Suite 40000, New York, NY 10013

ALL RIGHTS RESERVED. No part of this book may be reproduced in any form without written permission from the author, except for brief passages included in a review appearing in a newspaper or magazine.

COVER ART BY RUSS CLOWER

Leventhal, Stan, 1951-
    The black marble pool : a novel / by Stan Leventhal. —An Amethyst Press 1st ed.
        p. cm.
    ISBN 0-927200-05-8 : $8.95
    I. Title.
PS3562.E8734B57 1990
813'.54—dc20   90-563
                                                                    CIP

This book is dedicated, in memoriam, to:

Lou Dehnert
John Sturman

ONE

I was away from home, and even though I was supposedly working, it was like vacationing in paradise. Sunshine, cool water, palm trees distracted me from the bothersome details of life. I was in a realm to which I'd never been before. Everything was beautiful and exotic, tinged with an edge of excitement. This was a deviation from the boredom of my existence. I welcomed the breakdown of order and predictability.

My daily routine is so inescapable that even when I don't have to rise at six-thirty in the morning, I get up anyway. It's habitual. On that morning, my first full day in Key West, I opened my eyes with a feeling of wonder and joy. The room was striped with pale yellow ribbons as the sun's rays floated through the partially opened slats of the Venetian blinds. Moist, salty air filled my lungs as I stretched and the first distinct thought of the day began tripping along the network in my brain. I realized that the hosts and the other guests of Captain's House were probably asleep—unless they were still carousing.

After showering and shaving I slipped into shorts, a tanktop and sandals. The house was enveloped in a breathless hush as I moved through the dark hallway, across the living room, and opened the sliding glass doors that lead to the patio and pool. On the wooden planks of the deck I felt a million drops of perspiration collect on my face. Breathing deeply, I wiped my forehead with my palm and started the coffee maker, the main feature of the outdoor kitchenette.

As the perking sounds began and the stream of dark

brown liquid began to fill the pot, I put on my sunglasses and moved to the edge of the pool. I was not planning an early swim, just to dip my hand into fluid cool.

But it took several seconds for my eyes to convince my brain that something was awry. There was no water in the pool. And I was certain that there had been the night before when Pearl—one of the owners of Captain's House—had taken me on the tour. And besides being dry, the pool contained a corpse, its head in a puddle of brown blood, its arms and legs askew like a human swastika: the body of Walter Burgess. I didn't know his name at the time, nor did I know his face or reputation. He was a dead stranger. I assumed he'd been a guest at the house, and that he'd been murdered. Accident and suicide had not yet presented themselves as possibilities.

I looked down at the body of Walter Burgess and my brain stopped. Some kind of sensory overload must have frozen me. Divided between assessing the evidence before my eyes—empty pool, dead body—and deciding what to do about it—notify Pearl, call the police—I just stood there, mute, not thinking, like a mannequin in a window afraid to participate in this thing called life.

I don't know how long I stood there just staring, motionless, a cold grip on my spine from neck to lower back. But eventually, I backed away from the edge. Sat on a lounge chair under a striped awning. And waited for someone to come along and rescue me from my chilly trance. The sky and its gentle breezes, the ascending sun, the backyard fence were all as indifferent to me as I was to them.

Finally, two possibilities presented themselves: I could go back to my room and remain uninvolved. Or I could stay and get entangled in the aftermath of whatever it was that had happened. Having discovered the body, surely I'd be placed on the list of suspects.

Why did I stay and accept the responsibility of participating in Walter Burgess's death? Perhaps somewhere deep inside I was afraid that if I returned to my room, somehow it might be discovered that I'd been at the scene and had fled. This would look highly suspicious. Modern police methods are so very sophisticated—according to movies and television—that there is probably some device which could prove I'd breathed the air by the pool within a specific time of Walter Burgess's demise.

But maybe those kinds of fears had nothing to do with it. Perhaps I was just bored enough to be looking for some kind of entanglement. Something to engage my imagination. I'd never been involved in a murder before. Subconsciously, I may have said to myself, wow, a murder, how thrilling! And one never knows whom one will meet during a murder investigation. A handsome cop. A mysterious lady.

I sat on the chair beneath the awning by the pool, waiting for someone to come along and share my discovery. Maybe, by participating in whatever would happen I could fill the blank spaces on the questionnaire that is my life.

Pearl appeared shortly after I discovered the body. I would estimate that she's in her sixties. Thin, with very tanned skin stretched taut over delicate bones, an aureole of very white hair surrounding her face. When you see her move—slowly, with caution—she seems as fragile as a Ukrainian Easter egg. But when you hear her speak, in a voice full of experience and passion, you realize that there's quite a lot of energy and power in her deceptively small frame.

She wore faded cut-offs, a white T-shirt and a silver bracelet. "Good morning," she smiled, moving toward the coffee maker. "How's the water?"

I didn't know what to say. "Good morning," I finally blurted. And what was I supposed to say next? Oh, the water's fine—except for the corpse. Or, what water? Short of delivering a long, solemn eulogy (and I hadn't even met the guy), I couldn't think of anything suitable. So I rose and joined her at the kitchenette. After she prepared her cup, I fixed mine. Then I waited until she'd sipped. I'm never sure what to say to people I don't really know. And it had been less than twenty-four hours since I'd met Pearl Curran.

"I guess the pool was emptied since yesterday evening," I said.

"Oh, no," she countered, then smiled and looked at me like I was joking.

"It's empty now. Of water," I added, as tactfully as I could. And not wanting her to die of shock at the sight of the mangled body, I said, "It looks like somebody had an accident." I was full of anxiety as I said this. Perhaps Pearl had a heart condition? Would unexpected bad news create a serious problem?

"Really," she said diffidently, and moved toward the pool, her coffee mug still in her hand. I waited breathlessly as she got closer to the edge. Would she drop the cup? I came up behind her. I'd catch her if she fainted.

"You're right about the water," she chuckled, leaning over and looking down.

"Holy creepers!" she said as I reached out to hold her. But she didn't waver or fall. And her voice didn't sound surprised or shocked, just curious. She crouched, silently staring. Had she been expecting this to happen? What was her relationship with the deceased? Was he more than just another house guest?

"Are you all right?" I asked.

"Doing better than Walter Burgess, I can tell you that. Guess I'd better call the police. You wait here."

She disappeared into the house. For a few moments I stood there, like a jerk, not knowing what to do. Then it occurred to me that one of the reasons I'd come to Key West was to get some sun on my white fish-belly skin. And some warm rays were just beginning to shine on the deck by the shallow end of the pool. I returned my coffee cup to the sideboard, slipped off the tanktop and stretched out to wait and see what would happen next.

The sun always makes me light-headed; not quite dizzy and not quite stoned. It's a pleasant sensation if I don't overdo it. This can lead to a headache. But when it's right I can just let my mind go to wander and probe, poking into areas usually left unexplored. Daydreams seem like actual memories that I've experienced; fantasies are like movies that peel off the screen and wrap me up in warm and cool sensations. Sometimes my mind will wander into taboo territory and remind me of ghosts and demons that I prefer to ignore. But a fast escape back to the sweet realms of ambrosia is easily accomplished.

I'd not yet started to enter that intoxicating phase of sun-worship when several of the other guests of Captain's House began to materialize. At the time I figured I'd barely get to know any of them. So, at first, I admit, I was not too

10

attentive. Their names and faces seemed to enter and exit my brain like the latest news report. But eventually I did get to know some of them.

The first to show up for coffee—after Pearl and myself—was Frank Fiore: fortyish, dark, curly hairweave and a trim physique. Not a terrific face, acneed and angry-looking. Next came Edward Mallinson: mid-thirties, handsome with a palpable air of self-assurance, the kind of smile that generates confidence, straight, brown hair. And then, Skip Dunnock: blond, somewhere in his twenties, a hunk, boyishly masculine. Before he spoke he seemed very distracted, but his words hinted at a keen intelligence.

Not wanting to explain everything to them, I decided not to mention the corpse. I'd wait until asked. After I joined them in the shade of the awning hanging over the kitchenette, we chatted about our vocations. I could feel, very strongly—that sense of power and control, knowing what my companions did not. Or did they? Perhaps one or more of them were involved somehow in Walter Burgess's demise. I felt like I was playing a hazardous game as I sat, smiling, acting pleasant, wondering who knew what.

Frank, from Boston, is an executive with an insurance firm; Edward owns a bar and a disco in New York; Skip studies marine biology at a university in California I'd never heard of.

The only significant information I learned from them that morning was that all of them had been staying at the guest house for over a week. I assumed that they all knew Walter Burgess, at least casually, and that one or more of them might have some insight into the manner of and reason for his death.

The police put in a personal appearance. Pearl led them out to the patio and introduced us. We were each interviewed—privately—and told to notify them before leaving the island. They interrogated me in the living room. There were two: Officer Simon was very hot, sexy, with a moustache and rugged good looks, Officer Griffith was a little older and less attractive.

Officer Griffith asked the questions. I dutifully looked him in the eye while answering, all the time wishing that Officer Simon had been making the inquiries. I tried to imagine

Simon with his clothing removed. The image looked very appetizing.

When I told them that I'd only been on the island for less than a day, had spent the night in my room, alone, and had never met the deceased, I think they figured I was not connected. But I was certain they'd keep track of me just the same. After the questions pertaining directly to the body in the pool, Simon asked, "Are you here for any reason other than vacation?"

"Yes," I replied, watching him very closely.

He looked at me with impatience. I waited for him to tell me exactly what he wanted to know.

"What is your occupation?"

"Journalist."

"A reporter?"

I seized the opportunity to lock eyes. "Music critic."

"What kind of music?" He looked perplexed. I glanced at the perspiration stains on the armpits of his shirt.

"Whatever the head of the music department doesn't want to cover, I have to deal with."

"So, you came here to write about music?" He scrunched up his face in disbelief.

"No. Actually, the travel editor of the paper promised the local business group that we'd do a feature on Key West and he was going to come and do it himself but he had a family crisis at the last minute and I really needed to get away for a while so I offered to come and write the article."

It took every ounce of my strength to keep my eyes from Simon's crotch. I wanted to sneak a peek but didn't dare lower my eyes.

Griffith closed his notebook and said, "I see."

"Thank you for your time," said Simon, deadpan.

I smiled. He almost smiled back but looked away at the last second.

The interview was over. I was free to do anything I wanted so I returned to the pool.

TWO

I fetched a towel from the hamper on the deck and claimed a lounge chair. The hot, damp air made me feel lazy. My thoughts wandered with no direction, finally settling on a few points: I had to shed my New York skin and wriggle into the Key West mode of life. I wanted to have some fun. I had to write a dumb travel article. I wanted to get laid.

So I thought of my prospects. Of the three houseguests whom I'd met, I targeted Edward Mallinson. The closest to me in age, and the sexiest. I wanted to explore his body for a few hours; or at least to the point of orgasm. If I could only succeed in bedding this man, I felt that then I could return home to my lover, Paul, and bring a new level of passion and interest to our relationship.

It had grown stale. I suspect neither of us had intended to ever adopt a completely monogamous routine. But in the horrifying face of AIDS hysteria, we decided to live together and forsake all others—sexually. But it wasn't working. I can't say for certain whether Paul felt the same exact way, but I missed the variety, the mystery, and yes, I'll admit it, the danger of those fast, anonymous couplings which I'd grown so devoted to during the ten or so years after I came out. If I could just experience a moment of the old excitement, I would return to Paul, ready to assume my role as dutiful, faithful companion. I couldn't bring myself to sneak around with Paul in close proximity. As long as we were in the same town it would constitute a betrayal. But with the safety of distance, I allowed myself to do what would have been unthinkable on home territory.

Someone—probably Pearl—must have switched on the outdoor stereo system. Synth-pop bubbled from the speakers placed strategically on the fence surrounding the backyard. I opened my eyes, shadowed them with my hand, and observed Frank, Edward and Skip preparing themselves for sun-worship. They stretched towels over lounge chairs, massaged themselves with sun block and arranged beer, cigarettes and Walkmans on small, round tables.

"You ought to put on some sunscreen," said Frank, holding the tube out to me.

"You're probably right," I said. "But later. I don't want anything to get between myself and the sun just yet."

"I know what you mean," he said. "We northerners appreciate ol' sol in ways that these southern fried babes never will."

I nodded and closed my eyes. Didn't want to appear too friendly with Frank while Edward was around. Might screw up my plans.

I wondered if I should reach out to him—verbally—as Frank had done to me. Offering to grease his back might be too blatant. But silence might communicate an aloofness I did not want to convey. I waited for Edward to say something to which I could respond—pleasantly, intelligently—that might clue him to my desire.

But no words came from his lips. He attached his earphones to his head, closed his eyes, and kept time with his big toes. Perhaps, if I could ascertain what he was listening to, I could comment on it. The best consequence of being a music critic is that if you keep an ear open to all areas of the music industry you can find something to say to anyone as soon as you've pegged his or her particular tastes. Of course, there are some people who don't ever listen to any kind of music whatsoever. At least, consciously or actively. But most demonstrate a healthy auditory interest in something (even if it's only 'cause the lead singer is cute) and this provides a good handle for preliminary interfacing.

I looked over at Skip; trim, youthful, sexy, but too young for me. Then at Frank: good body, but his face...; and Edward: mature, handsome, apparently stable. He'd be perfect if we could find a common area of sexual interest. While not quite vanilla, neither are my proclivities ultra-kinky. I hate to think of myself as center-of-the-spectrum, but I guess, sexually, I am.

Earlier, while we were being interrogated, the body of Walter Burgess had been removed on a stretcher by some medics. Then, Aurelio, the houseboy, scrubbed away the blood and viscera with disinfectant. And Pearl refilled the pool, running hoses from all of the faucets on the first floor. As the water rose to the top, I was able to get a very good look at the pool.

When you first notice it, something seems a bit unusual. Then it occurs to you that most, if not all, of the pools you've ever seen before were painted blue or white. The Captain's House pool is black. Not painted black. But constructed of black marble and black tile. The marble has streaks of white that look like lightning bolts in a black sky. There is a sexiness to this pool; a personality. It looks and feels like a warm, wet blanket, surrounding and protecting you like a dark, quiet womb.

I continued sunbathing. Edward, Frank and Skip close by. Aurelio monitoring the rising water. Eventually, our intermittent, fragmented conversation turned to the subject of Walter Burgess.

"How about a dip?" Skip asked Edward.

I realized I wasn't the only one who had the hots for him.

Edward pulled the earplugs off and said, "Are you joking? After what happened?" He stared at the pool and a look of revulsion crossed his face.

"It's all cleaned up now," Skip persisted, diving in.

"Still," said Edward.

"No big deal," said Frank, rising from his lounge chair, diving in. He swam to the far end with a breaststroke, then butterflied back to the shallow end. "See? Water's fine."

"Still," said Edward, determined to flaunt his disapproval.

"How well did you know him?" I asked no one in particular, just to see who replied and what was said. I was not yet ensnared in the search for the killer. I was simply curious and had the subconscious desire to converse.

"A little," said Frank.

"Never met him," said Skip, emerging from the pool.

"Hardly," said Edward.

"Was he attractive, handsome, sexy, a nice guy, any of the

15

above?"

They paused to consider their responses.

Skip spoke first, spreading his legs wide, his Speedo creeping up his thighs to afford Edward a better view of his crotch bulge (or did I just imagine this?). "We were introduced but never talked or anything. Not super-attractive but not bad-looking."

Frank added, "He was always yakking about his tricks. According to him, every time he left a bar or disco he had the best-looking hunk in tow. Nice guy, though. Kind of quiet when he wasn't bragging." He kicked away from the side of the pool and executed a perfect surface dive.

"I hardly knew him," Edward reiterated, "but he seemed pleasant enough."

I attempted to catch Edward's eye, to see if I could detect any interest. But he didn't look at me. I glanced at Skip whose eyes were on Frank. Then I looked at Frank who had his eyes on me. He emerged from the pool. Dripping wet, he looked better than he had dry. He stretched out stomach-down and laid his head on his crossed arms.

I tried to think of some hook to engage Edward in a conversation before he put his earphones on again. "You said you were in the bar/disco business?" I inquired.

He turned to me, shielding his eyes from the sun. "Yes. There's one on Fire Island and one in Manhattan."

"It sounds interesting," I said.

"And you're a reporter?"

"Yes."

"That sounds interesting too."

I couldn't ask him for a date just then, with the other two in hearing range. I waited.

The remainder of the afternoon passed slowly. The heat and humidity were almost overwhelming. As the sun began to descend, we headed back to our rooms. I made an effort to try to engage Edward's attention on our way up the stairs but he ignored me.

As I was fitting my key to the lock of my room on the second floor, someone came up behind me. Frank.

"Would you like to come to my room for a beer?"

I did some fast thinking. I wanted Edward but might never have him. Frank was obviously available. I wanted to get laid by someone other than my lover. Fuck it, I said to myself, Frank ain't so bad. Besides, he might make up in technique what he lacks in aesthetic perfection.

"Okay."

When we got to his room on the third floor, he'd closed the door behind us, but he didn't offer any beer or indicate in any way that he might be interested in sex. His room was different from mine. Softer, the pattern on the bedspread a delicate filigree, the lighting from the lamps subdued.

"I just wanted to tell you," he said in a half-whisper, "that that twinkie Skip lied when he said he barely knew Walter. I saw them coming from each other's room several times. They were definitely more than casually acquainted." He punctuated this speech with a knowing look.

"Why are you telling this to me?" I asked.

"You seem curious."

"I am, sort of."

"And I had to tell someone."

"I see."

If I had to pinpoint the moment when I changed from disinterested observer to active investigator, it was probably then. I couldn't help wondering why Skip would lie and why Frank felt compelled to divulge it.

We chatted for a few moments about how beautiful the house was, how wonderful our hostess was, how adorable Aurelio, the houseboy, was. I strained my senses to pick up any covert body language or innuendo. But Frank seemed distracted and aloof.

I returned to my room, my curiosity growing. Why had Walter Burgess been murdered? Who had done it? Why had Skip lied? Why had Frank confided in me? What about Pearl and Aurelio? Were they part of some diabolical plot? And Edward? Was he as innocent as I?

I could not escape these thoughts. They circled round, pecking at my brain. My concern gradually shifted from my libido to my curiosity. Both wanted satisfaction. One would have to wait.

I lay down on my bed—a big, square thing—then got up to turn on the ceiling fan. I lay down again. And tried to nap.

When I'd first arrived at Captain's House I knew nothing about the place. But as my time there increased I learned a little of its history.

Like many of the older homes in Key West, the design is a hybrid of colonial, Caribbean and southern styles. Some of the buildings look like small plantation mansions. Others are like sylvan bungalows. There are verandas, porches, anterooms, and porticoes. Palmettos and vines surround these domiciles, cuddling them like nests, offering privacy and lovely views.

Around the turn of the century there were many ships about the Keys which were no longer serviceable. Some had simply outlived their usefulness. Others were crushed on reefs and rocks. Enterprising builders salvaged the wooden planks from these ships and utilized them to construct sturdy homes. Despite the many hurricanes that come and go, these buildings hold fast.

Upon entering Captain's House, there are rooms to the right and left of the front hall with a staircase straight ahead. Nautical prints adorn the walls, twine throw rugs with tassels lead past the stairs to the living room, adjacent to the kitchen. Beyond the sliding glass doors at the back of the house are the pool, jacuzzi and outdoor wetbar with kitchenette. Everything is decorated simply and tastefully, with none of the clutter that one finds at so many guest houses.

On the second floor are another three rooms, each decorated individually. One has a large canopy bed, another twin kings, mine, a huge square-shaped thing, unlike any bed I've seen before. Each room has its own motif, style, colors, mood. On the third floor are three more rooms, two of which have oddly-shaped attic windows and lower, slanted ceilings. In keeping with the rooms below, each has its own flavor.

The house was a private residence, owned by the Curran family, for the first sixty years or so of its existence. In the early seventies Pearl Curran, great granddaughter of Theophilus Curran, a rum-runner, inherited the house when her mother died of old age. With all of the upwardly mobile gay men traveling to the island for quality vacation time, Pearl decided it would be wise to convert her home into a guest house for men. She got a friend, a silent partner, to invest in publicizing the venture.

Their timing was perfect. As the island's popularity and reputation increased, Pearl reaped the profits of this new wave of tourist dollars. By the time the 1980s were almost over, Captain's House had become one of the most successful businesses on the entire island.

When the travel editor at the *News* told me he needed someone to fill in for him in Key West, and I told him I'd be glad to, he said, "You're gay, right?"

"Only when I'm not morose," I quipped.

He chuckled. "Then you have to stay at Captain's House. It's the best. Trust me. I'll call Pearl. Pearl Curran. She's terrific. A tough old dyke with a heart of gold. You'll love her. I'll make all the arrangements."

I napped for a while, and awoke feeling slightly chilled. I turned off the fan. Half-memories of nonsensical dreams drifted in my mind. I realized I was ravenous. The images started to fade. I whipped out my Key West travel guide to find a restaurant. After deciding on an outdoor cafe called Victor's, just a few blocks away, I dressed—ultra casually— and left the house.

With small tables beneath tall palms festooned with Christmas tree lights, the place was dark and quiet. My preferred milieu for dining. Particularly when alone. Sometimes I like eating by myself. At others I'm desperate for company.

But I sipped white wine and ate some well-prepared pasta while my thoughts focused on the matter of the murder at the guest house. I was already too enmeshed—in my mind, anyway—to forget about it. And, as I was deciding whether to order some coffee, I couldn't help but overhear a conversation taking place behind me.

I admit it. I listened in. Eavesdropped. But only because I heard the name "Walter" and, of course, my ears sent a message to my brain and my brain rang one of its many chimes which told my ears to continue gathering information.

When I'd arrived at the cafe I'd noticed the other customers, but none had seized my curiosity or interest. At the table next to mine, sitting behind me, were two women— middle-aged, nicely dressed and coiffed. Attractive. One was a little more buxom than the other. Her brown hair, curly, tendrilly and over-styled. The slimmer, prettier lady had sort of frosted blonde hair in twin waterfalls about her face.

I didn't, at the time, know who said what.

"We haven't seen Walter since the day before yesterday— I'm wondering if he caught on and went back."

"Naw. He's probably just partying somewhere. Or sleeping it off."

"Sometimes I just want to go over to that house and march right in and demand to see him."

"Don't."

"I won't."

"Good."

"Okay."

"Check?"

"Good idea."

They left a few minutes later.

At the time I wasn't certain that they were talking about the Walter at my guest house. It simply presented itself as a possibility. But later on I found out that they were, in fact, referring to the dead man in the black marble pool.

I ordered coffee and asked for the check. Within a short time the night people would emerge from their shells, float from bar to disco, slither about the dance floor, find a suitable partner for the night, then return home to fuck. It was years ago that I lost interest in staying out late, getting drunk, working up a sweat to a monolithic beat, to finally lap at the genitals of a complete stranger. But, I thought, perhaps that I'd be missing something by not participating in this kind of ritual. At home it would have been unthinkable. In Key West it seemed mandatory. At least, to attain a sense of having blended with the crowd and taken advantage of all there is to see and do.

I went to a bar called Woody's; typical leather-western ambience with lots of guys poised somewhere between desperate and aloof.

I went to a disco called Streets; lots of gay men and a handful of lesbian and straight couples whooping it up beneath glitter balls or cruising from the sidelines.

Apparently nightlife hadn't changed much in the ten or so years since I stopped. When I realized I wasn't missing anything new I decided to return to Captain's House. It was too early to go to sleep, but I figured I could read for a while, or better still—get a start on my article.

Walking back I began to think of titles: *Key West—Party Headquarters of the South; Key West—Fun In The Sun;* then my thoughts became sinister: *Key West—Pools of Blood; Key West—Murder at the Guest House.*

I was about two blocks from Captain's House. The moon was like a big disco ball, the air was heavy with magnolias and honeysuckle.

A figure approached me on the sidewalk.

Skip said, "Hi. You going back?"

"Yes. Think I'll call it a night." Stupid expression, I admit, but I use it all the time.

"Would you like to come to my room first? I want to show you something."

There was no trace of irony in his delivery. I couldn't imagine what he wanted of me. Unless this was a seduction. In which case I'd have to give serious consideration. He was a bit young, but very sexy. Something told me to try to measure the importance of his request. "Can this wait until morning?"

"No."

I followed Skip into the house, up the stairs and into his room.

THREE

After Skip unlocked the door we entered his room, a bit smaller than the others I'd seen. The four-poster bed had a gleaming brass headboard and crocheted coverlet. The weathered plank walls and circular windows gave the impression of a ship's cabin.

"Sit," he said.

As I lowered my butt to the bed, he searched through a gym bag. He pulled out swim trunks, T-shirts, sweat socks, bandanas and jockstraps, windmilling them into the air like a crook going through a rich lady's lingerie in a '40s movie. Triumphantly, he produced a notebook, thin-ruled, side spiral, rather thick.

"Read this," Skip commanded, sitting alongside me, placing the thing on my lap.

"Now?"

"Not right this second. As soon as you can."

"What is it?" Experience told me that it was either an autobiographical novel—probably heavy with sexual couplings, or a collection of poems—long on sentiment.

"You'll see."

I was in no great rush to read the collected literary works of Skip Dunnock and wondered if I could turn this encounter into something memorable. I sat there on the bed, casually, waiting to see what his next move might be. Might he pounce? Should I? Whisper sweet nothings? Tentatively brush his thigh? Was he just sitting there waiting for me to do something?

I cautiously leaned toward him and was about to drape

my arm around his shoulder when he stood up, cleared his throat. I almost lost my balance and fell off the bed.

"Well," he said, "I'm meeting someone at Streets. Got to run."

My passion—aroused and roaring, deflated and simpered, spiraling down like a pricked balloon.

"Okay," I said, trying to peel the bits of rubber from the floor. I tried to rearrange the pieces into an airborne thing in my mind, holding it aloft like an emblem of dignity, and ambled to the door with the notebook under my arm.

"Let me know what you think," he said earnestly.

I wanted to escape as quickly as I could. But I couldn't pull my eyes from his tousled brown hair, innocent face, lithe, solid body. I tore myself away with a fast "g'night" and tried to grasp whatever pride I could as I descended the stairs and fit my key to the lock.

On the bed. Ceiling fan whirred above. Sweat on my face like a damp washcloth. The breeze from the fan cooled, then dried the perspiration.

Previously, I hadn't wanted Skip. In the presence of Edward he'd appeared too young. But without the competition of maturity and wisdom, he became almost irresistible. I'd wanted him and he'd turned me down and I felt like a loser.

I tried to ascertain what lay at the heart of my desire. Was it his face, his physique, his youth, or simply the potential of a warm body? Any warm body. In those taut moments when I wanted to throw my arm around him and he moved away, was it Skip that I really wanted? Or was he merely a surrogate for what I couldn't have?

I don't understand the nature of attraction. Probably because there are no absolutes. If you can be disinterested in someone at ten o'clock in the morning, then crave their attention and affection several hours later, what does this say about you? Am I fickle? Or practical? Or just desperate?

There are certain faces and bodies that stimulate my gonads from ten feet away. There are certain personalities that do the same, regardless of the physical structure in which they reside. If there is a simple or reliable way of figuring out why I'm attracted to someone at a particular time, it remains a mystery. To me.

If Skip expected me to read his poems or novel, why hadn't he completed the sales pitch and had sex with me? This is America. You suck my dick I read your manuscript. Happens all the time.

I tossed the notebook on the floor. Curled into a fetal crouch. Drifted like a jellyfish from wave to wave. My Melville fantasies kicked in. Pretty sailors cavorting below-decks while cruel captains and scheming first mates used hard bodies for their selfish pleasure; inflicting wounds, currying favor, toying with the pecking order of rank and beauty. I saw tough men being tender with each other. I saw men brutally take one another with abandon.

The images that had begun in the North Atlantic sea, like the travels of Ishmael and Redburn on their maiden voyages, gave way to the Caribbean setting of buccaneers. I saw parrots on the shoulders of pirates, smelled hot, spicy rum, heard boisterous voices in a sing-song patois, tasted salty flesh as I pressed my body to the warm solidity of a randy sea-dog.

I awoke. Stiff and sweaty. Tight neck muscles. Cramped left calf. Showering helped. I didn't shave. Looked at Skip's notebook on the floor; at the paperback I'd started on the plane. Left the notebook where it was and took the novel—Anne Tyler—down to the pool. With sunglasses on, lying stomach-down, I read as the sun rose over the fence. As it ascended, the house sprang to life as bodies piloted by red eyes gathered by the pool. Steaming mugs of coffee. Aurelio made breakfast. I watched him. He was adorable.

Edward sat next to me at the table beneath the awning. Skip joined us. Then Frank. Aurelio scrambled eggs, buttered muffins, patted grease from bacon, fed oranges to the juicer, fixed more coffee, seasoned home-fries. Pearl netted flotsam from the pool with a long-handled scooper. We were the average American family breakfasting by the pool.

The one topic of conversation in which we could all participate—Walter's death—was not mentioned. At first. Skip commented on the weather. Edward lamented that he'd have to be heading home in a few days. Frank said he'd had the best time of his life the night before—playing pool at Woody's, then dancing at Streets until it had closed.

Pearl ate slowly, small amounts, infrequently administered. With the deep lines in her tanned face and her mane of white hair, she seemed like a reservoir of mystery. Without provocation or warning, she fixed her gaze on Aurelio and said, "The police are finished in Walter's room; you can clean it up today. Couple of guys from Japan will be checking in this evening."

"Okay, boss," he grinned, and having been brought back to this reality, started eating with gusto.

Pearl sipped some coffee, wiped her brow and said, "On the evidence so far, the cops can't be certain if it's murder, suicide or accident. Until something new turns up, the case is on hold."

I quickly scanned all the faces before me. To whom would this be good news? Bad news? Who would be indifferent?

Skip glanced at me, then stared down at his plate.

Frank shook his head, "So unfortunate."

"Yes," said Edward, "unfortunate. Tragic."

The remainder of the meal was consumed in silence. Afterward we sprawled about the deck. Sunning, reading, crossword puzzles, tanning lotion, Walkmans.

Eventually, I splashed into the pool. I'd been avoiding it. The sacrilege of playing in a makeshift tomb. But I had to overcome this fear, so, putting my reservations on hold, I plunged in. It was so cool and enveloping. Diving under, I swam to the far end. When I came up for air, Skip dove in and swam toward me. When he got to the end he propped his elbows on the deck and whispered, "Did you read it yet?"

"No, not yet. Haven't had the time. By the way, why is it that you think writers are interested in your diary or your poems or your novel or whatever?" I guess I was still miffed that he hadn't tried to seduce me.

"It's not mine," he said indignantly. "It's Walter's."

"Huh?" I must have rejoined, totally confused.

"It's Walter's journal. I got it out of his room before the police searched it."

I recalled that Frank had said that Skip had lied when claiming that he barely knew Walter. Why then, would he be in possession of Walter's journal?

Just then, Frank plunged in and swam toward us.

"Why did you give it to me?" I asked, hoping to get an answer before Frank reached us.

25

"Read it. You'll see."

He swam away and left the pool.

I listened to Frank yak about his insurance company for a while, then excused myself and returned to my room.

The house was so quiet it was almost scary; the kind of silence that portends evil or disaster. I entered my room and shut the door. Picked up the journal where I'd left it on the floor. As I opened to the first page, my breath came quickly, as though I was about to discover some deep, complex secret. But before I could read the first word, I heard a knock at my door.

"Who's there?"

"Aurelio. You want me to clean now or later?"

I opened the door. He stood in the hall looking like a doll waiting to be played with.

"You can come in now and do it if you like," I said, returning to the bed, picking up the notebook. Aurelio came in and closed the door behind him.

"If you're too busy now I can come back later," he said.

I looked him up and down. Moppet curls surrounded a virginal face. Nicely-shaped, solid but graceful, mocha arms and legs. Flat stomach. In his shorts and tanktop he looked about sixteen. I found out later he was twenty-one.

"If it's best for you now I can just..." I didn't know what I would do or where I would go if I had to vacate the room.

"Now or later. Whatever you want whenever you want it," he grinned. Slyly.

Was he propositioning me? Or was my imagination succumbing to the bombardment of horny enzymes?

Aurelio sat on the bed. I looked down at him with lust in my soul. I wondered what to say to someone so young. Then I recalled that once I'd been that young and back then it hadn't been a problem. A sure sign I'm aging. Then I asked myself why I was getting crazed over a kid. Because he was adorable. But he was probably a scummy hustler who'd demand money from me and break my heart.

The warmth in my soul turned to ice. "Why don't you come back later when I'm not so busy," I barked, not really meaning to sound so harsh.

Aurelio, with his eyes to the floor, left the room without responding.

I closed the door and felt like shit. Sat and lamented for him and myself. And eventually reined in my self-pity and picked up the notebook.

Then the telephone rang. Most guest houses don't have phones in every room. Pearl doesn't miss a trick. I picked up the receiver. It was Josh, the travel editor of the *News*. This was Saturday. At two o'clock in the afternoon. Same time as in New York. Why was he calling me?

"How's the weather?" he asked.

"Perfect. What's it like up there?"

"Freezing! Colder than the proverbial witch's tit and all that..."

"How's your brother doing? He was going into the hospital for..."

"He's holding in there. But it's so depressing and scary... that's why I called. I'm trying to get my mind off it. Figured I'd call to see how your trip was, how the article is coming along."

I had placed the article so far from the center of my consciousness, it was shocking to be reminded.

"Oh," I must have stammered, "fine, fine."

"Did you speak with the Chamber of Commerce people?"

"Not yet."

"The tourist bureau?"

"No."

"The photographer I told you to call?"

"Um, no."

He lectured me about my vast responsibilities as a travel correspondent and his enormous chore to make certain that travel writers did not abuse the many privileges of their sacred task. If I didn't turn in one fucking great article he would exact his fucking ton of flesh by reporting me to the fucking editor-in-chief.

I sat there thinking: sure I'll write a great travel article. But there are other things going on here which are a bit more thrilling. Besides, they wouldn't fire a music critic for an unacceptable travel piece. Or would they?

I told Josh everything he wanted to hear. Said goodbye. There, under the influence of guilt, I placed the journal on the bureau and left Captain's House to take notes for my travel article: *Key West: Sun, Sand & Sex.* Then I thought:

27

Key West: Murder, Mystery, Mayhem. And *Sex.*

There is one main thoroughfare—Duval Street—which runs the length of the island. By the time I came to the intersection I'd forgotten all about Aurelio and his extra-curricular enterprise. And I didn't give a thought to Walter Burgess. I'd never met him, knew nothing about him, and didn't care about him at all.

I passed one lovely house after another. Each set back from the street, each nestled in a bouquet of tropical verdure. The styles are eclectic—like taking a film studio tour and passing from the set of *Gone With The Wind* to *Key Largo.*

But Duval Street is all-American, Anytown, USA. All retail window displays and facades are designed to attract the eyes of upwardly mobile young professionals raised on television. Everything is bold day-glo colors offset with glass and chrome; angular, sharp, bold, screaming for attention, changing rapidly, these stores would not be out of place on Columbus Avenue in Manhattan. Or, on the television screen in your living room. Most of the merchandise is not utilitarian, nor is it meant to last very long, nor is there an item lacking a well-publicized designer logo. Away from Duval Street one can find an occasional small, less ostentatious, independent venue with a stock both useful and practical. But in the center of town, competitive marketing and impulse shopping prevail.

I was glad I was wearing shorts and a tanktop. But still, I was damp with perspiration in the seven or so minutes it took to get from the house to main street. I reminded myself of the pad and pen in my rear pocket. And I set off in search of something wonderful to write about.

I passed an old theater with a Hollywood deco facade, a shop with bright, hand-painted T-shirts, and an emporium that sells nothing but over-priced junk. I placed pen to pad and jotted these things down, hoping that these words would later inspire a grand aria when I switched on my word processor.

The sights beginning to bore me, I glanced at the sky. Peaceful. Clear. Quiet. Pink clouds in a cerulean setting.

Then I turned my attention to the people. The locals could be from any small, southern town. Casually dressed, slow moving, all charm and friendliness on the surface. Extremely polite to the tourists, they sometimes say nasty things about them to the other natives. America. The visitors don't act like they're in a small southern town. To them, it's like San Juan, Acapulco or Bermuda. With their fashionably tortured hairstyles, expensive leisure-wear and mania for accessories, you'd think they were visiting another planet.

I perused some postcards in a tourist-trap notions outlet then glanced up to notice Officers Griffith and Simon harrassing a homeless person.

The difference between New York and Key West, besides the thousand or so miles, is that at the southernmost tip of Florida you don't have to worry about winter. I was shocked when I realized that the homeless problem isn't restricted to the big cities. I never imagined that a classy resort town would have sidewalk residents and alley-dwellers. But after spending some time in Key West it seemed so obvious: if one is to be without shelter, better a warm, tropical place than the bitter winds and inescapable cold up north.

The guy was very young, skinny, tanned, longish hair and wild eyes. Griffith prodded him with his nightstick. Simon nudged him with his shoe. Too unsightly for main street. The kid struggled to his feet and wobbled down the sidewalk. The cops watched him moving away, then resumed their patrol.

I watched Simon's trim, nicely-proportioned body swagger up the street. From the rear he looked appealingly sturdy: substantial calves, meaty thighs, taut butt, slim waist, broad shoulders. I turned away before anyone might notice me staring.

Then I saw the two women whom I'd overheard at the restaurant. I decided to follow them. See if "their" Walter was also "my" Walter. See if I could stay close enough to maybe catch a bit of their conversation without being detected.

Both were about the same height—a bit shorter than me—the darker-haired one more broad and bouncy. The blond, a wispy thing, looked like a starving fashion model. At the time I had no idea what their names were, but I subsequently learned that the darker, heavier one was Regina Carson and the lighter, slimmer one was Joyce

Burgess. They both wore pastel shorts, white cotton blouses, sandals, broad-brimmed hats and carried shoulder bags. The newness of their apparel and accessories bespoke their status as tourists.

They touched hand-painted T-shirts, tried on outrageous sunglasses, argued about stopping in at a dress shop. Joyce was all for it. Regina claimed that they weren't there to shop for things that could be found back home. Where was home? I didn't know yet.

Then they went to a restaurant. A simple place without a theme or gimmick, and ordered iced-tea and English muffins. I tried to get a table in close proximity, but was unable. When they departed I followed, keeping what I believed to be a safe distance. They walked away from Duval Street, passing the house of Ernest Hemingway. After taking a few pictures, they continued walking. I couldn't get close enough to hear anything. The next stop was the Monroe County Library. A few more snapshots. And then, to my surprise, they walked to Captain's House. But stood on the opposing sidewalk and just looked at it. They whispered a few things to each other. I recalled that one of them had said something about entering a house. Could this be the house to which they referred? Why were they just standing there looking?

I waited until they left, then went inside. As I leapfrogged the stairs to get to the room I told myself that the answers to all of my questions were probably very neatly written out in Walter's journal. All I had to do was read it, satisfy my curiosity, give it back to Skip and get on with my travelogue and vacation.

But when I reached my room I discovered it was gone. Nowhere in my room. I searched everywhere: under the bed, under the rug, in the closet, on the night table, on the bureau. I wondered who might have taken it? Probably whoever killed Walter Burgess. But I had no idea who that might be. And who knew I'd had it, apart from Skip?

I decided to take a nap, try to forget all of the unexpected complications I'd been confronted with. It would soon be Saturday night and I was ready to go out, party hearty, have a joyous and memorable evening.

FOUR

I took a nap, dozed dreamlessly, then prepared myself mentally for a night of wild partying.

But that was before I attempted to get out of bed. My back, chest, arms and legs felt hot and tight. Movement brought pain. As I sat up and threw my legs over the side I realized I'd gotten too much sun. And switching on the light, I saw that my skin—usually so pale—was pinkish red, a sure sign of too many ultra-violet rays. I walked, or jerked, actually, in a rather stiff and comical fashion, to the bathroom. A hot shower would hurt but ultimately relieve me slightly. I stood there, teeth clenched, hot needles stabbing my tender skin. Total torture. But I did feel better afterward. And better still after applying some lotion.

I prepared for a wild night of disco madness. A pair of excruciatingly tight jeans, faded and worn in all the right places; a white sleeveless T to show off the marvelous color I'd taken such pains to acquire; a new pair of white high-top sneakers. Although these look best on a teenager, a thirty-five year old like myself can get away with it if he hasn't put on too much weight and isn't too tall.

Working up all the courage I could, I went to the bathroom again and faced the mirror. Always a sobering act. I suppose some people can't wait to get to a mirror and enjoy every moment in its presence. But I dread it. Not blessed with flawless skin and exquisitely sculpted features, I don't have an impressive portfolio when it comes to face value. Some faces earn their owners millions of dollars, megatons of adulation, clamoring hordes of admirers. Mine is one that is

31

instantly forgettable and not about to be of much use to anyone unless I commit a crime in which case it will be used to identify me so that I can be captured and brought to justice. It's not a terribly ugly face, just not memorable, exciting or irresistible. If the world did not place such a large premium on face value, I would probably be a bit happier. But I've learned to accept reality and deal with it as best I can.

I have pretty good hair, though. It's brown and curly and looks acceptable most of the time. So after lamenting my face I combed my hair which helped me to forget about my face. I was in fairly jovial spirits when I finally left the house to join the rest of America for its weekly Saturday night jamboree.

With the scents of jasmine and wisteria in the air, the night was cool, fresh, inviting. I was rolling along with a saucy gait, nothing troubling my mind when I suddenly thought of Paul. And wondered if he was sitting home, lonely, remaining faithful to his true love who was in Key West all set to commit adultery. I felt bad for a few moments. Then guilty. Finally a wave of shame swept over me like a tsunami.

My steps slowed. I almost stopped and contemplated returning to the house. There was an article to start; a stolen notebook to find; a murder to solve.

But then I asked myself when I'd ever have another chance to act young and single and foolish again on a Saturday night in Key West? The answer was maybe never. And what if Paul wasn't sitting quietly at home, but was on his way to the same kind of action I was seeking? I believe in faith and trust and fidelity. But I also believe that opportunities are meant to be taken advantage of.

My pace accelerated and I headed for the center of town, the confluence of nightlife in Key West. After a drink or two I'd completely forget my reservations and have a swell time. Of this, I was certain.

My first stop was Woody's. Didn't want to plunge too quickly into the turbulent currents of a disco. I figured I'd ease myself slowly into the standing puddle of a bar and then, acclimated, dive headfirst into the Sargasso that is a modern dance floor.

Every medium-to-large city in America has a bar like Woody's. Dim lights, smoky air, the suggestion of mystery and danger, pool table, video games, loud music, horny men. The customers are usually of the butch variety; lots of leather and denim, very little of this year's fashions. The men are friendly except for the occasional attitude-monger and mostly quiet, except for the occasional screechy laugh that rises from the crowd like a butterfly, flashes its wings like semaphores and then disappears. The music in such places ranges widely, usually with a heavy emphasis on oldies, R&B, C&W, and R&R. The first thing I heard was Loretta Lynn; then Sam and Dave; then the Jefferson Airplane. I felt right at home.

Neither of the bartenders looked very appealing to me. But scattered about the pool table was a collection of interesting possibilities. Some people look first at the eyes or face. Others are interested in biceps and torsos. My particular interest is further down. It's the jut of the butt, the curve of the crotch, the sighs of the thighs as they struggle against the confinement of tight, faded denim that makes my heart race and my palms sweat.

So I kept my eyes on a few potential prizes and waited for an opportunity. The danger of waiting for opportunities is that while you're marking time, others are targeting you as one of their opportunities. And while I watched a cute, sexy number lean over the pool table and sink the eight ball, a guy whom I'd immediately dismissed from my agenda came to my side and introduced himself.

His name was Howie and he was nice. Not very attractive though, according to my standards. He was too skinny for one thing (toothpick thighs) and his hair looked like it hadn't been washed since the Civil War. But we chatted for a while, amiably, until he asked me what I did for a living.

"I'm a music critic."

"A critic?" he asked, as though I'd said Nazi rapist. "I have a real problem with critics," he said and proceeded to regale me with all of the times television movie critics had said unkind things about movies he'd liked. I wished to pursue the conversation and him no further. I bade him farewell, and because I felt the need for a change of milieu, left Woody's and headed over to Streets.

Except for the huge pink and green flashing neon sign, it's a fairly nondescript building. Could be a warehouse, except for the sign. Outside is a box office where you pay the cover charge and get your hand stamped; ropes on stanchions to control the lines of people waiting to get in; and two doormen—one tough and one pretty—to give you a sample taste of the kind of attitude you can expect on the inside.

As soon as you've entered you can hear and feel the pounding of the beat. Electric bass boosted to inhuman decibel levels. There are potted palms and murals of tropical, Rousseau-like scenes. And men. All shapes and sizes. All ages and proclivities. Cute southern boys with tan skin, urban tourists with sunburns, Hispanic boys in white T-shirts, many from the Caribbean and Central America. And the occasional straight or lesbian couple.

The dance floor—not as large as a football field, not as small as a doormat—is surrounded on all four sides by long bars, each with three or four bartenders. As in most discos, the bartenders are incredibly beautiful, amazingly stupid and astonishingly haughty. These requirements have become so standardized I believe that anyone who fits them can be certain of finding this kind of employment.

Behind the dance floor is another world, an emporium of entertainment, a whole other realm to explore. First there is the room with silent porn movies on TV screens, then the pool table room which leads to the video game arcade, adjacent to the outdoor bar and cabaret. Somewhere within this labyrinthine maze is an indoor cabaret and a restaurant. But I could never find them. I'd ask directions, they'd point and mention rights and lefts, I'd follow as closely as I could, but I never arrived at the intended destinations. This did not distress me too much, though, because the dance room, dirty movie room, video arcade and outdoor cabaret were quite enough to keep me amused. I never missed the other stuff.

After briefly scanning the occupants of these rooms, I returned to the dance area and ordered a drink. My eyes roved from figure to figure as I assessed the crowd. Searching for sexy bodies and familiar faces. There were plenty of the former. And being new in town, I saw few of the latter.

But eventually I spotted Frank, then Edward, and later on, Skip.

As I stood there, caught between the Scylla and Charybdis of nonchalance and eagerness, I drifted into a memory vortex. Images of disco nights past swirled around my cerebral cortex like ballroom dancers. My first night— Twelve West in the mid seventies. It was like a secret club that I had to maneuver, angle, scheme and connive to get into. I plotted, lied and called in favors to gain entry. Inside, the beat wrapped itself around me like an expensive fur coat. There was that strange, intoxicating aroma, poppers and sweat, permeating the air, reminding me of the scent of men's bodies after sex. All those handsome, well-built young men. Their shirts dangling from rear pockets, their chests moist, warm, smooth. They whooped and hollered like aborigines at a frenzied, primordial ritual. I joined without hesitation, like answering an ancestral call. When my hips caught the rhythm my mind seemed to fly into the stratosphere. Thoughts were rapid and crystalline. Nothing worried or bothered me. My arms and legs felt free, finally, as though pardoned after a protracted incarceration. I didn't meet a single soul. Danced by myself that first night. And felt like I'd transcended the boundaries of space and time.

But then, this grew into a routine. I'd find myself night after night at the same disco, dancing to the same songs with the same people. The excitement diminished. Eventually I couldn't stand to be at one of those places. Not for a minute. Finally I stopped going altogether.

Now, when I'm out of town, away from the crushing intensity of New York's nightlife, I will occasionally go to a disco. And I wonder why it's still such a phenomenon. I see guys my own age or thereabouts, who apparently never stopped. Who've been dancing all these years. Why didn't all these people get bored like I did? What are they still doing here? Are they the sane and normal ones, or am I?

As time continued pacing forward, Streets began to get crowded. I wandered from room to room looking, watching, searching. Trying to make the best of a Saturday night. Frank was passing through the video game arcade and he spotted me near the pool table. He wore designer jeans, creased, an alligator shirt and Topsiders. He looked like

35

someone trying to dress "gay" but not quite knowing how. If he'd been a bit more fashionable or a touch more scruffy, he would have been far more convincing.

As he approached, I braced myself by finishing what was left of my drink.

"Quite a crowd," he said, grinning like an idiot child.

"Yes."

"Would you like to dance?" he leered. What he meant was, do you want to fuck?

"No thanks," I said. "Maybe later. I'm still getting used to being here. Haven't been inside a disco in over a year."

"Disco is alive and well in Cleveland," he said. "I've been going to the same one for years—Galaxy—have you ever heard of it?"

"No. Never have. But I've never been to Cleveland so I don't know much about it. Everything's changed in New York. No more Ice Palace, no Studio, no Saint. History. Only a bunch of new places I've never been to."

"You New Yorkers are too damned much!" Frank's eyes blazed and his complexion grew crimson. "You expect everyone to know everything that's going on in your city but you make no effort to find out about anyone else's."

"Gee, Frank, I really didn't mean to offend you," I said, not certain what had unleashed this display of anger. Was he upset because I wouldn't dance (fuck) with him, or because he really hated New York and its denizens? "But I'm awfully tired of people telling me how nasty New Yorkers are, how we have such bad attitudes and whatever. I've met just as many obnoxious people from all over. New Yorkers don't have a monopoly on anything."

I guess he wasn't expecting such an outburst from me. My words and tone told him he'd better back down unless he was prepared to debate this to some sort of conclusion. But being the diplomat that I try to be, I spared him the ordeal of making a decision and simply changed the subject.

"Frank," I said, "why did you tell me that Skip lied about not knowing Walter?" I was already referring to this dead man whom I'd never met by his first name. Like we'd been pals.

"Because, strangely enough, you seem less involved than anyone else and you also seem to be the most concerned."

"What do you mean, less involved?"

"Well, you never even met him. In fact, technically, it was all over for him before you arrived."

That got me thinking. All over for him before I arrived. Maybe Frank knew something. Perhaps he was involved, or dare I even think it, the culprit? With caution, I pressed on.

"And what do you mean, most concerned?"

"Every time his name is mentioned your ears perk up and you get this look in your eye."

"What kind of look?"

"Curiosity."

I must have flushed scarlet. I tried to rationalize my behavior and said something like, "Oh, I didn't know it was that obvious. But well, I guess, to tell the truth, it is kind of fascinating. I've never seen a dead body before. And I just love murder mysteries." I tried to sound as innocent and naive as I could. I didn't want him to know that I'd been making mental notes, following people around, asking questions and had actually had my hands on Walter's journal.

I hoped that Frank had perceived my response as guileless. But I was frightened: what if he was the murderer and he thought I suspected him? I felt shivery chills doing a slow tango up my spine. There I was, standing and talking to a possible murderer. Maybe Frank knew about the notebook? Perhaps he'd stolen it from my room? I attempted to be as cool and casual as I could. "Too bad about Walter, though," I said with as much empathy as I could. "Too bad I never had the opportunity to get to know him." I shook my head slowly to demonstrate my regret. Then, as smoothly as I could, sighed and said, "Well, I'm going to ambulate and see what there is to see. Later."

"Later," he smiled, and I moved away from him. Quickly drew up to the nearest bar and ordered another drink. My hand shook as I brought the glass to my lips. I sucked the whole thing down instantly. And felt a bit better as fluid fire radiated into my extremities.

I went to the edge of the dance floor. If I didn't look too desperate or disinterested, someone might ask me to dance. Someone sexy and interesting.

But no one requested my company. I watched Skip dance with a very attractive body builder. Finally heard a song I recognized. Decided to pick out a handsome stranger, ask him to dance, see what would happen.

Nothing. I spotted a hunk—intelligent-looking face, trim physique with interesting bulges—walked over and asked if he wanted to dance? No. Did he want a drink? No. Did he want to talk? No.

I got another drink. And wandered around. Saw Edward, looking great. Chiseled face, sculpted body, hard nipples punctuating tight muscle shirt, alluring basket-buns-thighs combo. I didn't dare approach him. He'd treat me something like an elephant does a tsetse fly.

I was getting loose and clumsy, but decided to have one more. Most of it wound up all over my shirt. I realized I'd had enough. Left the disco and headed back to Captain's House.

Duval Street was rain-spattered. Tiny drops of wetness, darker than the dry spots, made everything look temporary. As I moved through the deserted streets the rain came harder and faster. My initial impulse was to run because in New York you must be very wary of catching colds. But in a climate like that of Key West the rain and air are so warm, getting drenched is like making love. It coats your body like soothing creme while it electrifies your nerve endings. The heightened sensitivity you feel during sex is replicated in a warm, balmy tropical rain. Almost like bathing in the jism of God.

I slowed my pace, enjoying the impact of every raindrop. The fresh air and water on my face sobered me. My hair became plastered to my forehead and tiny rivulets ran down my nose and cheeks, tickling me. If I couldn't have sex at least I'd have warm rain and I'd appreciate it.

I was about three blocks from Captain's House, passing a small plantation-style manse, approaching an alleyway, when a voice, in a stage whisper, said, "Hey!"

At first I ignored it, of course. In New York when a stranger addresses you you don't stop to see what he or she wants. You just keep going if you place any value at all on your life and your time. So I just kept walking, as though I hadn't heard anything. Then, again, "Hey!"

Footsteps tapped lightly on the sidewalk. "Hey!" Louder and more insistent.

I stopped. Turned. Peered through the increasingly heavy rain. It was very dark. A figure came closer.

Officer Simon stepped from a shadow. He smiled. "Goin' home?"

"Yes," I said, thinking I'd use the rain as an excuse to hurry away. While I wondered what he wanted of me, a playful smile appeared. He stared at me, almost grinning. His clothing was soaked through like mine, but the wet fabric of his khaki shirt made his magnificent torso stand out in high relief. I stared at him. His eyes seemed to talk to me. Like a jolt of electricity to my brain, I received the message that he craved some kind of sexual release. He took my hand and led me down the dark alley, tall houses on either side. Beneath my feet I felt gravel. Then we reached a patch of grassy weeds. We faced each other. In the dappled dark I looked at his face, serious now. He touched my cheek and wiped the rain from my forehead. I didn't wait for any instructions. Getting to my knees, I unzipped his regulation suntan khakis and stuck my fingers inside. A million butterflies emerged from his trousers. They fluttered into the rain and washed away like a pastel drawing on a wet sidewalk, the colors running and bleeding like a Jackson Pollock. Closing my eyes, I saw Catherine wheels and Roman candles. I took his cock in my mouth and sucked like a starveling.

The scent of his musky crotch, the taste of his salty skin, the water running down my face, my back, his soft moans, his muscles responding. I kneaded his warm, meaty buns, rubbed his sturdy thighs. I could feel him growing harder, longer, hotter. Then it was over. I licked my lips after greedily swallowing. And rose to face him. He had a faraway look in his eyes. Turning away, I emerged from the alley and returned to Captain's House. In my room I thought of Officer Simon's butterflies, only a hallucination of course. But the sex had been real. I could still taste it. I felt content, almost blissful. Carefree and loose, I arranged myself on the bed and drifted into the dark and dry warmth of slumber.

FIVE

I slept like a contented child, obliviously, nothing cruel or harsh invading my sense of all-consuming bliss. And I awoke, the taste and smell of Simon still fresh to my senses. Unlike the usual me who can't wait to get started and jumps out of bed immediately, I lounged, dozed, trying to hold onto what I could of my moment in the rain.

Hunger finally drove me from the bed and into the bathroom to prepare for breakfast. But while showering and shaving I began to think about Paul. Actually, I felt guilty. I'd cheated. Committed adultery. Betrayed his trust. Guilt overrode the hunger so, before going downstairs I called home. But Paul didn't answer. The machine picked up. I left a brief, sweet message. Then looked at my wristwatch. It was only 10:30. Sunday morning. Paul should have been home. Maybe he'd gone out and spent the night with someone. I can live with that, I told myself. Then I considered the possibility that maybe he was taking a shower or a shit. And therefore couldn't come to the phone. This latter scenario was far more comforting. I pushed Paul away from the center of my consciousness and dressed to go down for breakfast.

Aurelio was there. Pearl too. A young black woman I couldn't identify. And the two Japanese visitors I'd heard mentioned previously.

The sun shone brightly. There was no sign of last night's rain. The black marble pool was silent, its surface smooth. It knew everything but revealed nothing. Looking at it shimmering in the sun you'd never guess that it had been

40

used to kill someone.

The young black woman was named Janis. When Pearl introduced us she didn't say, this is my lover. But it didn't take me long to assess their relationship. Older woman with money. Younger woman with beauty. A timeless arrangement.

Janis is easy to describe, in physical terms. She's got very long limbs, a tiny waist, and small, beautifully shaped breasts. Her hair is cropped close and spiky, her complexion is dark brown with red highlights, like mahogany.

Her intellectual, spiritual makeup is more difficult to define. She has an air about her that implies she knows more than she'll ever tell. And she has a calm, peaceful disposition as smooth as camomile tea, with a hint of turbulence just below the surface.

I was introduced to the gentlemen from Japan, but, to be honest, I can't remember their names. Difficult to pronounce and spell. Having just recently come to grips with Hispanic names, I'm beginning to get a handle on the Asian variety.

Their English vocabulary consisted of a dozen or so phrases from Berlitz and some sexual phrases they'd picked up from translations of gay porn magazines from America. Since I don't know a word of Japanese, except of course, sushi and sake, we didn't talk much. And consequently I never got to know them well. But they were pleasant and friendly. Both always smiling and nodding enthusiastically. Perhaps it was my imagination but they seemed to regard America as some kind of holy shrine. I got the impression that their trip to Key West was like a pilgrimage to Mecca. They were fascinated with my sunglasses, Edward's Walkman, Skip's running shoes. None of these items were unusual to them, obviously. They seemed to be studying how we used them, handled them, regarded them. I guess so they could return to Japan and then do the same, like an American going to Paris to see how the rich women accessorize their expensive new clothes.

But after being with the Japanese for a few days, I realized that it wasn't America or American ways that intrigued them. It was American homosexuality. They wanted to be as hip, with-it, groovy and up to date as the typical American gay guy, I gathered, so that when they

41

returned home they would be the cynosure of their local bar or disco. If there was some question as to what the typical American gay man was having for breakfast, dancing to, reading or wearing, these two would have all the answers, and the authority of empiricism, to impress their friends. I'm certain of this because it's the same whenever a friend of mine returns from a theater week in London or a museum tour of Florence.

Janis cooked breakfast while Pearl read the mail. I assumed, by the volume and the fact that I'd not seen her do this before, that she let it accumulate during the week and dealt with it all at once on Sunday mornings. Aurelio lounged in the sun while the Japanese guys scanned copies of *Torso* and *Honcho*, the first things they'd purchased upon arriving in Key West.

After breakfast, Aurelio went to work cleaning rooms, Pearl and Janis washed the dishes, the Japanese guys went sightseeing with their cameras.

I stretched out on a lounge chair, smeared sunscreen all over. I felt like Superman. Still glowing from my encounter with Officer Simon. This experience made me feel better about myself. Like I was actually desirable—or dare I even think it—sexy. So tangible was this feeling that when Edward came down to the pool a while later, I was able to strike a pose of nonchalance that I would not have been capable of previously. And this made all the difference in our relations. Now that I'd attained some measure of satisfaction I was no longer so desperate. My attitude, body language, and vibrational aura did not scream at him with expectation. He became friendlier. Apparently, when you want something too badly you won't get it. But as soon as the craving diminishes, just try to get away from it.

"I saw you at Streets last night," he said, "did you have a good time?"

"Great," I said. "My most memorable night here so far. You?"

"Oh, it was all right. I've had better times, worse times."

He slid a cassette into his Walkman. "What are you listening to?" I asked.

He stood right next to the chair where I lay. Taking off his shirt, folding it, stretching out on his back less than a foot away from me. I could smell him. His gym-hard body and even tan caused a stirring in my Speedos.

"Pet Shop Boys."

"They're pretty good," I said and then decided to toy with him a bit. "Did you know that Neil Tennant used to be lovers with George Michael? Of course, that was before the relationship with Morrissey."

This little lie seemed to have the desired effect.

"No shit!?!"

"Well, that's what Neil told me last time he was in New York. Of course, he was a little high at the time and he might have been exaggerating. Or maybe he was just teasing me. You know how those British rock blokes can be. But I believed it."

To say that Edward was impressed with my insider information would be the understatement of the century. He started plying me with all kinds of questions about English pop stars. Which ones are gay? Who's had who? Did I think Bronski Beat would ever reunite?

I enjoyed every bit of his attention and deftly tossed him fake crumbs which he gobbled up like a hungry pigeon. I felt very grand and superior when I told him I'd have to interrupt our conversation because I'd had enough sun and needed to go indoors. But, if he wanted to continue talking sometime, that would be possible.

"How about dinner?" he asked.

"That would be great."

"Tomorrow night?"

"Fine."

I gathered my things and returned to my room.

Aurelio was there. Making the bed. I entered cautiously. Hoped there wouldn't be a repeat of our last encounter in my room. I was trying to indicate that I was not angry with him, but also, that I still wasn't interested in playing any games. In attempting to maintain this fragile balance, I felt nervous, vulnerable. I greeted him. He said hello. Then I spotted the notebook—Walter's journal—on the night table. My mind raced across the possibilities and when it got to Aurelio a buzzer sounded. Perhaps he'd taken it, read it, and returned it. He had a key to my room. No one would question him about coming or going to or from any room in the house.

But that would make it too obvious. He'd be a complete fool to think that he wouldn't be suspected. And if I accused him, he could simply deny it and I wouldn't know any more than I already knew. I didn't want to insult him, in case he was innocent. So I just kept quiet. Pretended nothing unusual had happened.

"Would you like me to come back later?" he asked, no emotion betraying his feelings.

"That's all right," I said. "Finish now. I'll just sit here and wait until you're done." I opened my Anne Tyler—I was dying to read the journal but didn't want anyone to witness my desperation—and sat in the easy chair by the window. Started reading.

But I couldn't concentrate. All I could think about was Walter, his death, his journal, who had taken it, and why had it been returned? And then I got a little crazy because it occurred to me that Aurelio might think the reason I sat there while he worked was because I didn't trust him and had to stand guard. It seemed to me that I couldn't have been any less tactless if I'd put a gun to his head and demanded to know why he'd stolen from me. But I couldn't get up and leave. Too obvious. He'd think that I knew that he knew that I knew. Besides, I was so anxious to get my hands and eyes on the journal I felt like I might explode. And Aurelio took his time. He moved so slowly—picking up a pillow, changing the case, fluffing it up, arranging it just so—I wanted to throttle him and shout: Do you think you might finish before the turn of the century?

But I kept quiet. Did my best to pretend I was absorbed in the book. And felt my blood pressure rising every second as Aurelio dusted the bureau, fetched clean towels, vacuumed the floor. I could have done the entire job in three minutes. He'd already spent over half an hour.

Eventually, finally, at last, he completed the task. Picked up the bundle of dirty sheets, towels, pillow cases, wash cloths. "See you later."

"Thank you, Aurelio."

He closed the door. I waited a second or two and sprang out of the chair so fast I almost knocked it over. Then tripped over my toe, went flying and crashed headfirst into the bed. Fortunately. Had it been anything harder I wouldn't have lived to tell anyone about it.

When I regained my composure somewhat, I got up. Seized the notebook and plopped belly-down on the bed. I began to read. And kept at it until I'd finished. It probably took me about six hours with a few occasional breaks. It was almost nine-thirty when I got to the end of the last page.

The notebook answered a few questions, but left me even more befuddled than I'd been before. At least, I had a starting point from which to launch a more focused investigation.

I sat on the bed in my room ruminating, thinking, meditating, trying to fit the pieces I had, the few that there were, into a larger pattern or design. Then the phone rang and I had to push these thoughts aside.

"Hello?"

"Paul, is that you?"

"Yes. I got your message but when I called you weren't there."

"So, how are you?"

"Fine. How's Key West?"

"Incredible. Beautiful. But listen, there's something I've got to tell you..." and I proceeded to tell him all about the weird murder and its aftermath. He listened patiently, inserting all the right uh huhs, oh reallys, no shits, and you don't says. But all the time I was talking and he was responding, what I was really thinking about was: what did you do last night and can you tell what I did last night.

When I completed my dissertation on Walter Burgess, concluding with the journal I'd just finished reading, I asked him what he thought.

"Sounds to me like you're jumping to conclusions. He might've committed suicide or it might have been an accident."

"But what about the stuff in his journal about passing? Seems to me that he was a sure-fire candidate for blackmail."

"If this is how you want to amuse yourself on your vacation it's fine with me. By the way, how's the article coming along?"

"What article?" For a moment I'd actually forgotten about it, so absorbed had I become in Walter's demise. "Oh, right, the article, *Key West: Sun, Sand and Sex*—I mean, *Surf*; it's going great, just fine."

At this point I realized our conversation was nearing a close. Should I ask him what he did last night? I decided not to. Nor did he ask me.

"Well, I've got to run," he said, "get some stuff ready for tomorrow morning."

"I love you."

"I love you, too."

We hung up. I sighed with relief. And my thoughts turned to Walter's journal.

Much of which was gibberish. There were long passages dealing with his business ventures and (I'm guessing) his personal fantasies—revenge, success, sexual, the usual. I had no trouble reading his handwriting, just trying to figure out what his words signified. Much was inaccessible to me. But juxtaposed with these sections were others in which several things were very clear: Walter had a wife, Joyce, whom he usually referred to as "wife." And he also had a lover, unnamed, whom he called "beloved." In addition, he was being blackmailed. But whether for cheating on his wife or for masquerading as a gay person, I couldn't tell. Walter was a heterosexual, to the bone, married with two kids, a mistress. He was not gay. Had never been. Nor had he ever "experimented." But he'd attempted, and succeeded, I gathered—in convincing all of his business associates that he was gay. Why would a successful straight businessman pretend to be homosexual?

This was the first question and I figured I might get an answer or at least find out where to find the answer, if I had a chat with Skip. It was he, after all, who'd given me the journal. My first priority was to corner Skip, find out what he knew and why he'd chosen to involve me in the perplexing quagmire that was Walter Burgess's death.

SIX

I went down to breakfast. Had a pleasant meal with Pearl, Janis, Aurelio, Frank, Edward and the guys from Japan. Edward reminded me about our dinner date that evening.

Skip never appeared. So I waited a while and knocked on his door. No reply. I knocked again and called out his name. Still nothing.

I decided to go for a walk. Just sitting in my room began to make me crazy. I didn't want to go down to the pool because I'd had enough sun.

I walked to Duval Street and wandered. Roaming down the sparsely populated, sun-bleached, steamy sidewalks, passing kaleidoscopic storefronts and cooking fragrances from the open doors of restaurants, eventually drifting into the residential area. My mind became like a stern judge: examining evidence, searching for morsels of truth, trying to make sense of the life and death of Walter Burgess.

I've learned that truth is central to life. Without it, everything gets too complicated and difficult to handle—like playing Jacob's Ladder with strings of glue. And somehow the truth itself is complicated and difficult. But somehow, an unwieldy truth is preferable to a comfortable lie. I guess because the truth leads to progress, the future, resolutions. Lies hold us back, prevent us from ever gazing at a clear, understandable picture.

It disturbs me when people lie. Or when I do it. But it has become one of the most acceptable facts of life today. In America, if your lies lead to wealth or renown, you are congratulated, celebrated, respected. This is unacceptable to me. Even though I am just as guilty as anyone. If someone asks me how I am, and I don't feel like explaining my stiff neck, sore knee, pounding headache, I lie and say, fine. This does no harm to them or myself. But then there are the serious lies, the devastating ones that obscure the true facts of life. The false pictures they create distort our perceptions and ultimately, our reality. The government, big business, advertisers and religious leaders all realize that it's in their best interest to keep the population as ignorant as possible. Therefore, more easily manipulated. And we willingly, knowingly, every day, accept lies from corrupt politicians, news broadcasters, advertising campaigns and in-the-closet celebrities.

This is America where lies are okay. So, it shouldn't have surprised me that Walter lied. But, why would he pretend to be gay? Rather an unusual twist, I thought. But realized that, of course, it probably had something to do with money.

My face was so sunburned by this time, I was trying to walk away from the sun, in the shadows of the trees, down the sidewalks with taller buildings (what few there were) to keep the harmful rays from my face. It was so hot my clothes were damp and sweat ran down my cheeks, tickling me, bringing a salty taste to my lips.

I turned a corner, crossed over to escape the blast furnace effect of the direct rays and saw Officers Griffith and Simon approaching.

My throat felt like I'd swallowed a tennis ball. If Simon said anything which referred to our brief encounter of the other night, what would I say? I was pretty certain he was in the closet. Wouldn't acknowledge that his dick had been in a man's mouth. Not in the presence of his fellow officer.

And I, of course, had a choice. I could be truthful and mention what a terrific time I'd had savoring his sperm. But this would embarrass him, probably get him in trouble and wouldn't exactly place me at the top of his list of favorite people. So I decided, regardless of what Simon did, I would be discreet.

They got closer. I tried to act like nothing unusual had happened. We were less than ten feet away. I looked at Simon. He looked right through me. Not a flicker of recognition.

"Good day," said Griffith.

"Hi," I said.

They passed me and I slowed. Then turned to see if Simon would glance back. He did. I smiled. He looked ahead and kept walking. I decided to go back to Captain's House. Perhaps Skip had returned.

Crossing Duval, I saw Joyce and Regina. Leaving a dress shop. Each had a parcel. They were dressed casually. Didn't look as wilted as I felt.

I'm not usually very bold. But something that I can't define took hold of me and suddenly, without thinking about it very much, probably because Walter's journal was still fresh in my mind, I walked over and started talking.

"Hello," I said, stepping up to greet Joyce. "You probably don't remember me, but we met a few years ago at Walter's club. Yes?"

There, I'd done it. After reading Walter's words I jumped to the conclusion that this woman was his wife. And I guess I had to find out if I was correct. At the time, it didn't enter my mind that I might be confronting a murderess.

"I don't recall your name, but your face looks familiar," she said.

I introduced myself.

"Joyce Burgess."

Bingo. "How's Walter?" I asked. And as I did, my heart swerved into the fast lane.

"He's fine. Back home. Very busy. I'm here with my friend Regina Carson—" we shook hands, "because Walter was too busy to get away."

"Are you having a nice visit?"

"Oh, yes, it's wonderful here."

"Wonderful," Regina agreed.

"Well, nice seeing you again," I said to Joyce, "nice meeting you," to Regina, and I walked away from them with all of the nonchalance I could muster. I wondered if she really thought she'd met me before, or if she was pretending to be polite, to throw me off of her trail.

When I got back to Captain's House I went to my room. I had to evaluate what had just happened before confronting Skip. Did Joyce really think her husband was back home? No, that was not true. The conversation I'd overheard proved that she knew he was staying at Captain's House. But, did she know that he'd been killed? Or had she done the killing and was now playing ignorant to protect herself? I couldn't know the answers to these questions, not yet. But one scenario presented itself, which, at the time, made sense: Joyce and Walter had come to Key West separately, one of them without the other's knowledge, most likely, for the purposes of spying.

And then the really big question presented itself like a neon billboard: did Joyce know that he was dead, or was she just pretending?

I realized that this thing was getting deeper and more complicated and possibly more dangerous than I'd ever imagined. I had to figure out what was going on, if for no other reason than to protect myself from this weird bunch, these people who apparently lied about their whereabouts, their sexuality, their marital status, their knowledge.

I went to Skip's room to see if I could find out why he'd given me the journal. Two knocks and I waited. Thought I heard something. "Skip!" I said. More sounds. The knob turned. The door opened. Skip stood in the darkened room, his eyes squinting, his hair like it had been styled with an egg-beater. He wore wrinkled white jockeys. And looked dazed.

"Sorry to bother you, but we have to talk."

"About what?"

"The notebook you gave me."

"Oh." It took him a while to gather his consciousness. "I need to take a shower," he finally said. "And some coffee."

"Shall we meet by the pool in about an hour?"

"Sounds good."

I sat in the shade by the pool. No one else was around. The sun was starting to set. It seemed a bit less humid than it had been. I felt a slight ripple of air.

Skip appeared in Speedos and a T-shirt. His skin was as burnished as Miles Davis's trumpet tone. At that moment, it seemed that if I were to touch his tanned, warm skin, it would be like caressing a jazz riff; the warmth, the sensuous vibrations.

He fixed himself a mug of coffee and sat beside me. His face looked pained.

"Are you all right?" I asked.

"Don't know yet," he said.

"Too much to drink?" I asked, teasing.

"Somebody drugged me, I think."

Or you took too many drugs yourself, I wanted to say. And he looked at me as though he sensed my disbelief. "Really," he said, almost pleading, "I think someone may have put something in my drink last night."

He sat and thought about it. Then asked, "What day is today?"

"Monday."

"What time?"

"About five."

"You're joking!"

"No."

"Someone must have drugged me on Saturday night and I slept from Sunday morning to Monday afternoon."

"Who? And why?"

"I was at Woody's just before closing and I was playing pool. Someone offered to buy me a drink. He went to the bar to get it."

"Who?"

"Can't remember his name."

"What did he look like?"

"Longish blond hair. Skinny. Tall. Bad skin."

"Nobody I know fits that description," I said. "Why would somebody want to drug you?"

"Maybe 'cause of Walter," he said, sheepishly.

I seized the moment to ask my questions. "Skip, this is important. You knew Walter, more than just casually?"

"Well, yes."

"Would you care to elaborate?"

"Not at this time."

"Why?"

"I might be accused of murder."

"I see. And why did you give me the journal?"

"To protect myself."

"You mean, something in the journal would absolve you of any wrongdoing?"

"Sort of."

"Why me?"

51

"'Cause you're a writer and you never even met Walter so you're completely uninvolved."

I couldn't help but chuckle. "There was a time when I was uninvolved," I said, "but with each passing second I seem to get more tangled up in this whole mess."

"Welcome to the party," he said sardonically.

"Can you tell me why Walter pretended to be gay?"

"Yes."

"Will you?"

"If you promise never to reveal what I'm telling you."

"Okay." I realize I'm violating my promise to Skip by relating all of this, but that was then and this is now and a lot has changed since Skip and I sat by the pool having this discussion.

"Walter owned a bunch of clubs in the early seventies—he'd inherited a lot of money and wanted to invest in what he called 'fun businesses'—clubs, restaurants, discos. Of course, he found out that running them isn't as much fun as it seems. Anyway, early seventies, gays are taking over the disco scene. Walter decides if he's going to have a successful disco he'd do better running the show if everyone thinks he's gay."

"How do you fit into this?"

"I'm not really a marine biology student."

"Really?" I said, trying not to sound too sarcastic. "You're a hustler."

"That obvious, huh?"

"Not really. I've just been slightly obsessed with this whole thing and it occurred to me as a possibility."

"Walter hired me to be seen with him. So people would think he had a boyfriend."

"You never actually had sex with him?"

"Right. He wasn't into it. Just wanted people to think he was."

"What about his wife?"

"Never met her."

"What else?"

"Well, at some point, I guess about two years ago or so, someone started blackmailing him."

"Who?"

"I don't know."

"Any ideas?"

"A few. But now that I think maybe someone's trying to kill me, I'm not saying any more about that."

"One last question. What were you and Walter doing here in the first place? Was this a business trip or for pleasure?"

He sighed. "He was negotiating with one of the owners of Streets, possibly to invest or buy him out. I'm not sure which. But that's all. Not another word. I'm going."

He rose, left his coffee mug in the sink and disappeared inside the house.

I went up to my room to get ready for my big dinner date with Edward. Then went down to the living room where I sat, reading a magazine, waiting. No one else was around. The house was still. I walked to the pool and sat beneath the umbrella.

SEVEN

The air seemed spiced with heliotrope. Dusk in the tropics. Moon shadows beginning to form, dark clouds drifting, swatches on the pool deck where light passed palm fronds. Quiet except for the cicadas. The breezes finally began to stir, eager for some motion after the laziness of the day. The pool was smooth and dark.

Janis came out. She wore short short short-shorts—what used to be called "hot pants". And a halter top. Her sandals dangling from her hand. She sat on the edge of the pool with her legs circling like propellers.

We talked. Drifting like plankton. She was waiting for Pearl to finish dressing. I waited for Edward to arrive.

Janis was twenty-two. Born outside of San Francisco. Named for Janis Joplin. "Mom, she wasn't very well educated. Never left Oakland. Still lives there. When Big Brother came along she heard them on the radio. She named me for Janis. It wasn't until I was about sixteen that I found out she was white. When I told my mother she didn't believe me. Thought I'd made it up just to hurt her. But we're okay now. Except that if she knew I was living with Pearl she'd probably freak right out."

She'd traveled to Key West with friends after graduating from high school. Met Pearl through a mutual friend. And had decided to stay. "I came here about two years ago and I haven't left yet. Not even for a day trip to the Far Tortugas. But one of these days I'll go back for a visit. But then I'm coming right back here. It's like paradise."

I wondered if she had any ambition. Or would she be

54

content to just help out around a guest house. She told me that someday she planned to write.

"Write what?"

"Screenplays. No one reads books anymore. Besides, all the money's in Hollywood. But I wouldn't want to be an actress or anything. Too much pressure to look good."

"But you look sensational."

"Thanks. But that's temporary. Anyway, wouldn't want to be a director or producer. Too much stress. I'll write the stories and let everyone else worry about turning them into movies."

It grew darker. The moon emerged from behind some clouds, then disappeared again. Tiny ripples moved across the pool as Janis paddled her feet. She asked me what it's like to be a music critic. I told her it's nothing like writing screenplays.

Pearl joined us. In a blue work shirt, pressed, white Levi's and a leather belt with a big brass buckle. She asked if I was enjoying my stay. Fine. How's the article coming along? Great. Janis rose from the pool deck, swinging her sandals by the thongs.

"Now you have to go back to the room and dry your legs," Pearl scolded.

Janis sighed with exasperation. "You know," she said to me, "Pearl was Janis's nickname."

"I know," I said. "I loved her."

"Janis who?" Pearl asked.

"Joplin," we said, simultaneously.

"Janis was telling me about how she was named."

"Hell," said Pearl, "first time I heard her I thought she was black too."

Janis walked, daintily, back to the house. Pearl followed. "Have a nice night," she tossed over her shoulder.

I was alone. But not for long. The pool and patio lights blinked on. Probably set to a timer. The dusky dark was now illuminated with feathery beams and twinkling points of light.

Edward appeared. He looked so good I was tempted to invite him up to my room. Forget about food. Familiarize myself with his nooks, crannies and protuberances. His hair lifted with a breeze. He looked suave. In the yellowish artificial light he could have been a European fashion model. He knew of a restaurant. Elegant but casual. From the outside it looked like a well-manicured Southern gothic domicile. Within it had the appearance of an English manor. Embossed wallpaper, cream with a gold trim. Candles in wall-sconces. Wainscoting and delicately carved moldings. There was the quiet hush of a gentrified gathering. Silverware gently tingled on china. Conversations and individual voices were indistinguishable. The waiters, all spruced and sharp, moved slowly, silently, among the well-spaced tables. Pinpoints of light glistened from just about everywhere.

We were seated at a large table with a centerpiece of fresh cut flowers. No water spots on the glasses. No mending stitches in the table cloth. We ordered drinks and Edward lit a cigarette. I looked at him with what must have been expectant eyes. I wasn't sure what I had hoped to accomplish with him. Was this to be a simple way for two strangers to pass some time while away from home? Would the evening end with us wrapped in each other's arms? Or would I get some important clues to help unravel the knotty questions surrounding Walter's death?

I didn't know what to say, so I commented on the beauty of the decor, the evocative atmosphere, the handsome waiters. When our drinks arrived Edward reminded me of who I was and why I was in Key West.

"So, you're a music critic who meets a lot of rock stars and you're moonlighting as a travel writer, right?"

"Right." I didn't want to tell him that I rarely met rock stars. That the travel piece I'd been assigned was as far from my consciousness as Ancient Tibetan Epic Verse.

"My work is nothing like yours," he said. "There's nothing very creative or exciting about it."

Relieved that we were to talk about him, I said, "What exactly is it that you do?" I recalled that he had something to do with discos and restaurants, or was it clubs and cabarets?

"You know the Tornado Club on Fire Island? Planet X in Manhattan?"

"Yes."

"I own them. Used to own a few others too. I'm here in Key West, vacationing, and scouting some locations. My backers and I want to cash in on the boom here."

As I sat there sipping vodka, listening to him, I felt a jolt to my brain. If Edward was involved in gay discos and restaurants, might he not have been acquainted with Walter Burgess? Might they have been competitors? Might Edward have blackmailed and murdered him?

I realized my face could easily betray these thoughts. I fought hard to prevent my eyebrows from rising, my mouth from gasping.

"It's not like it used to be, though. Ten years ago you could make a lot more money from the gay community. Now with so many people dying and more people staying at home, and more bigotry around, well, it's not as easy as it used to be."

"Easy?"

"Making a profit. With the rising inflation rate, the weakened dollar, the crazy tax situation—overhead is impossible and less people have money to spend on non-essentials."

I decided to risk asking a few questions that might help my investigation, but would not clue him to my increasing sense that Edward was a prime suspect. Immediately after Skip Dunnock.

"How long have you been in the business and how did you get started?"

"I borrowed money from friends of my parents and parents of my friends. I took out loans. Back then it was easy to get a loan if you had a degree."

"What did you major in?"

"Officially—business administration. Unofficially—sex, drugs and rock 'n' roll." He leered.

The waiter came to take our order. But we hadn't looked at our menus yet.

"Would you like to hear about the specials?"

We nodded.

In addition to their pasta, seafood, poultry and meat dishes, they were offering a lobster special, some kind of Oriental chicken, and barbecued ribs. There were all kinds of Southern specialties on the menu such as fried okra, hush puppies, cornbread, and candied yams.

I ordered the lobster and Edward asked for a steak. Lots of good trimmings accompanied the meal including cole slaw, salad, popovers and crudite.

When the waiter left, I started asking more questions. Loosened up a bit by then, I became bolder. "Do you know any other gay restauranteurs like yourself?"

For a moment his face looked strange. Like I'd startled him. But he quickly masked himself and stated, "I've met quite a few others—both gay and straight—but it's not like we have a secret network or exclusive club."

I didn't think that I'd implied anything about covert conspiracies. What made him react so unusually to this particular question? What was it that made him nervous? And then it occurred to me that I had no idea whether he was being honest with me. Had he been lying, how was I to tell? How was I to separate the intentionally misleading answers—the serious lies—from the trivial fibs that people tell each other every day? The only way for me to ascertain his veracity was to research his answers. So I took mental notes throughout the meal.

I'd check up on him as best I could.

Steeling myself, as if from the impact of a wrecking ball, I asked the most crucial question. My palms were sweaty and my heart danced a jig.

"You've been in the business for about fifteen years, Walter Burgess was too. Did your paths ever cross?"

Edward's face turned white. His eyes widened. He cleared his throat. "Well, actually, we may have met but it's not something I recall."

"Quite a coincidence that you'd both turn up at the same guest house just before he was murdered."

Edward made a silly grin. Had I gone too far? Or had he grasped what I was after and now that he knew, had decided to toy with me?

"Quite a coincidence," he said. "Remarkable." The sarcasm in his tone would have whittled a redwood. I tried not to let my discomfort show. At that moment I decided that Edward was the killer and he knew I was on to him. So I'd have to be very cagey. I figured, aside from the way his good looks intimidated me, I could easily maintain control over the situation since I was the good guy and he was the villain.

With a kind of leering smile, he said, "Well, we've done nothing but talk about me. Tell me about your work."

Just then the salads arrived. Bright red tomatoes, crisp romaine, cucumbers, alfalfa sprouts, green olives, red peppers and radishes. Mustard vinaigrette dressing. Yum.

"Well," I said, using my salad as an excuse to delay my response, "my work probably isn't nearly as exciting as yours." I wondered whether to lie and keep up the pretense of rock star buddies. Or own up and tell him just how boring and routine my work is. "It has its moments but it has its hazards too. Like if I review a loud rock group on Tuesday night, I can't tell if the string quartet on Wednesday night is in tune."

Edward looked astonished. "You review rock *and* classical?"

"And other stuff too."

"That's pretty unusual, isn't it?"

"Used to be. Less and less, though. I guess I'm a musical polymaniac."

"What's that?"

"Someone who's fanatical about music but not any one particular kind. I like everything—when it's good."

"Not too many of you folks, I'd imagine."

"More than you'd suspect. A lot are in the closet." When I said "closet," Edward blanched. I took note and continued. "There are a lot of people who pretend to enjoy something because they think it will get them into certain social circles, or because they think they'll get laid."

Edward smirked.

We ate in silence for a while.

Then Edward asked, "Why are you so interested in Walter Burgess?" The serious look on his face sent cold rushes down my spine, brought goose bumps to my arms. My appetite dropped to zero. Was I eating face to face with a cold-blooded killer? Would he do something dangerous or was I safe for the moment?

"Because it's intriguing. And I'm convinced he was murdered. And no one else seems to care."

Edward looked at me expectantly.

I pressed on. "His wife is here in Key West and she doesn't even know he's dead."

"Wife?" Was Edward truly unaware of this or was he protecting himself?

"Yes, wife. He was married, with two kids."

"Really?" he said, but I couldn't tell if he didn't believe me or already knew and was playing ignorant.

"Really. Apparently he was straight but pretended to be gay for business reasons."

"You seem to know an awful lot for a casual observer." More lines formed on his forehead.

I wondered if I should tell him about Walter's journal. Then decided not to. "Just curious. There's not a whole lot to do around here. Keeps my mind occupied."

Our entrees arrived and all I could think about was whether Edward was the culprit, and if so—was he now plotting my demise? I had no appetite and sort of dismembered my lobster in such a way that it would look as though it had been consumed. Edward's appetite seemed unimpaired.

We spoke very little during the remainder of the meal. He offered his opinions of Pearl—a sweet old lady; Janis—a pretty airhead; Aurelio—adorable; Skip—a foolish youth; and Frank—a nerd.

All the time we sat there, I pretending to eat, Edward forking and chewing heartily, I felt divided. I wanted to pleasure myself with Edward's maleness. And I wanted to denounce him—share my suspicions with the authorities. It was like holding two strands of twine, each supporting an anvil, running through a pulley and the flame of a candle. Beneath each anvil is an egg. The eggs represent the fate of humankind. I must pull or loosen each strand, as the moment demands, so as to protect those eggs from those anvils. My entire consciousness is engaged in successfully maintaining this difficult balance, protecting those treasures. The strain is enormous. But I can do it.

We had coffee and liqueurs. I was feeling the alcohol all over my sunburned body. It felt like I was floating in an airless vat of warm cotton balls. After arguing over the check we divided the sum, added the tip and walked back to the house.

As we made our way over the sidewalks I imagined at any moment that Edward might pull out a knife or a gun, shove me into a dark alley, and thereby prevent me from going to the police with what I knew. Or suspected. My eyes and ears were alert, waiting for the slightest surprise movement. When Edward reached up to sweep his hair from his forehead, my body stiffened and I was on the verge of bolting away with lightning speed until I realized all he was doing was brushing his hair.

When we got back to the house Edward asked, "Have you ever seen the pool at night?"

"Yes. It's beautiful," I said.

"Have you noticed how you can't tell whether it's full or empty with the lights on?"

"Huh?"

"Come, I'll show you."

The house was dark and quiet as we moved through the hallway, into the living room, out to the pool deck. We walked to the ledge at the water's perimeter.

Edward said, "Look closely. With the night lights just beneath the edge of the water shining into the pool, and the lights from above the awning shining onto the surface, it makes the pool look empty." He stopped and swirled his fingers in the dark water. And he was right. Before plunging his hand in, the pool had looked empty. Now, with the water rippling away from his wrist, it looked full. He took his hand out, the ripples stopped, and the pool looked empty again— like a huge, dark pit with nothing in it.

"Interesting," I said, wondering why he was pointing this out to me.

"I'm going to step inside and turn on a few more lights," he said.

I nodded. He left me and entered the house. I looked at the still water of the pool and waited for him to return. Any second, more lights would radiate and I'd feel safer.

Suddenly, I sensed something or someone behind me. Two hands pressed against my back and I plunged uncontrollably into the inky water. Just before my head went under I heard a voice say, "Go home! Go home!"

My mouth and nose filled with water as my hands and legs flailed to get myself right-side-up. But I was fully clothed and with my jeans clinging to my legs, plus the weight of my water-logged shoes and socks, maneuvering was difficult. Gasping for breath, my heart beating like a hummingbird's, I finally managed to get my head above the surface. Choking and spitting, blinking the chlorine from my eyes, I looked for Edward, assuming it was he who had pulled this practical joke. At least he wasn't trying to drown me. But no one was there. I turned 360 degrees but I was alone.

About ten seconds later Edward casually stepped to the edge of the pool. He grinned. "Couldn't wait, huh?"

I looked at him incredulously. "Third graders can think of more clever stunts than this one," I said, pissed off.

"What are you talking about?" he asked, spreading his hands in supplication.

"Ha, ha, ha," I said, all sarcasm. "You may be amused but I'm not."

"What are you talking about?"

"I didn't jump in. I was pushed."

"Not by me," he said, his grin fading.

I glanced around. "Who, then?"

He raised his palms to the moon. I was attempting to climb out but my wet clothing made it difficult. As I struggled, I developed a head-to-toe case of goose bumps. Not from the cool night air. What if it wasn't Edward? What if someone else had crept up, pushed me in and then disappeared? But who? And who would demand that I go home?

"Thanks for a lovely evening," I said, weakly attempting to hide my anger. I trudged up the stairs and entered my room. Removed my wet clothing and toweled myself dry. Then plopped down on the warm, comfy bed. I closed my eyes but couldn't sleep.

EIGHT

I lay in my bed, my mind racing out of control. Got up to make certain I'd locked the door. Went back to bed. My muscles felt as though they'd been stretched on a rack and my stomach lurched like a trampoline. I breathed deeply, tried to settle myself. Then got up again and dragged the armchair to the door and wedged it beneath the doorknob. No one was coming into my room unless I invited them.

I got back into bed. Closed my eyes and opened them again. My brain was in overdrive and I knew I'd never fall asleep until I'd satisfied all of its demands. But the questions, problems, loose ends and nagging edges attacked me like moist-feathered, scaly-legged monsters. My first task was to organize them into a tame flock, from which they could address me in an orderly fashion.

But my first chore was to determine if I wanted to even attempt to deal with all of this. I had to ask myself: why have you let yourself get involved in something which doesn't concern you?

Perhaps it was simply out of boredom. There I was in a strange town, fairly strange, not one friend or acquaintance to hang out with, none of my home comforts to distract me. Suddenly there's a scandal. Oh boy, this will relieve the monotony. But, I had to admit to myself, I really hadn't been there long enough to get bored. Maybe it was because I discovered the body? Or because I wanted to avoid writing a stupid article? Could it be that my subconscious made a deal with my consciousness to allow the murder to displace the real job, which I probably, no definitely, did not want to do?

Is it a crime to become interested in a crime?

This may have explained why I got involved. But what was it that was keeping me involved?

When I think of all the reasons why I want to live, and all the reasons why I want to die, the live list is always a lot longer than the die list. So why was I participating in something that could possibly terminate my life? Perhaps because subconsciously I'd made a trade-off: that it was better to live a short, full, exciting life than a long, dull one? Is it truly better to burn out fast at full intensity, or shed a pale, flickering glow that lasts a long time but never illuminates very much?

I guess I opted for the laser and not the candle. Or else I wouldn't have been lying there in the dark trying to make sense of the shadows in my brain.

After determining that I would pursue my investigation to whatever ends it might lead me, I pushed on. There were clues to assess, evidence to examine, research to be conducted, notes to be organized and analyzed.

I turned on the light, got out my pen and legal pad. I started making lists and jotting notes to myself.

It must have taken me several hours to gather all of the information. Halfway into this project I reminded myself that I could easily resolve the entire situation by utilizing the Gordion Knot solution. I would simply return home and forget the whole thing. But by this time I was hooked. The answers to many questions were motivation enough to press on.

It must have been about six o'clock in the morning when I finally arrived at several conclusions and knew what had to be done next.

Oddly, I felt better. My muscles didn't ache anymore, my stomach was calm. But most surprisingly, my mind was fresh and clear. As though I'd slept soundly. The first glimmerings of dawn peaked through the windows. My room was a study in shades of gray.

I'd placed Skip Dunnock and Edward Mallinson at the top of my list of suspects. But I hadn't forgotten about Frank, Aurelio, Joyce and Regina. Just to be safe, at the bottom I added Pearl and Janis. Most likely, they had nothing to do with any of this, but I figured it wouldn't harm anything to be on the alert for suspicious vibrations from anyone with whom I came in contact. I'd read enough murder mysteries to know that, usually, when a homicide is involved, everyone is guilty until proven innocent.

Skip was the only one who'd admitted knowing Walter Burgess, but he'd allegedly lied, according to Frank. I had to figure out a way to ascertain Frank's credibility. And see what else I could find out about Skip.

Edward was in the same business as Walter, he had opportunity, possibly motive, and he'd reacted rather strangely when I'd broached the subject of Walter's death at dinner.

And suddenly I remembered that my room had been entered and searched, the notebook taken away and then returned. Who was responsible for this and why? Aurelio, Pearl and Janis certainly had the opportunity. But no motives that I could perceive.

Although I knew that it was dishonest, unfair, deceitful, illegal and immoral, I decided that what I must do was find any clues or evidence as to their innocence or guilt. This might be difficult to do. But then it occurred to me that if I plotted very carefully, I might be able to get Aurelio to help me. Perhaps, even, without his knowledge. I knew that this was wrong. But my room had been violated. My secrets were known to the intruder. My life was quite possibly in danger. Therefore I gave myself permission to invade Skip's and Edward's territories to protect my own.

I considered the name at the bottom of the list. Frank could be connected somehow, which would explain why he'd lied about Skip, if in fact, he'd lied. My instincts told me he wasn't involved. But Joyce and Regina. Why had Walter's wife and friend come to Key West at the same time as he did, behind his back? Were they spying on him? Could they have had something to do with his death? I had no idea. I decided to keep them on the list and try to learn as much about them as I could.

And who'd pushed me into the pool? Demanded that I go home? Pearl? Janis? Aurelio? Frank? Skip? Edward? Perhaps someone I wasn't aware of yet? I was fairly certain it wasn't the Japanese guys. But beyond that, I hadn't a clue.

After organizing my notes and lists, I hid them beneath the mattress. I lay down and closed my eyes. Just as I was drifting into slumber the telephone rang. It was 7:30 in the morning! Who could it be and what could he or she want? I picked up the receiver.

"Hello?"

"Loverman. It's Paul. Sorry to call so early but I wanted to catch you before you were gone for the day."

"What's up?"

"Nothing. I just wanted to talk."

"Oh," I said, relieved. I'd thought he'd called because of some dire emergency or something. But then, I thought, there must be something wrong. "What's happening?"

"Nothing in particular, I just wanted to say hello."

"Why did you call so early?"

"I already told you, I wanted to get you before you left." He was beginning to sound exasperated.

"But what is it that's so important that you had to get me before I left?"

"Why are you being such an asshole?"

"Me? An asshole? I've never been guilty of any such thing. Why did you call?"

"That's a good question," he said huffily. "I'll try to think of an answer and remind myself what it is the next time you're out of town and I miss you. Asshole."

Click.

He hung up on me. At the time I was furious. What kind of nerve did he have to, first, call me at a ridiculously early hour? Was he checking up on me? And second, why had he been so testy? Maybe because he could tell I hadn't slept, and assumed I'd been doing all kinds of sordid, adulterous things?

But looking back, I realize that I was truly an asshole. At that moment in time, during that particular conversation, I was the bad guy. Poor Paul had simply called because he loved me, and I'd twisted the conversation into a thing of suspicion and unnecessary nastiness. If I'd been as aware of my assholishness then as I am now, I would have made a point to phone him and apologize. But I did not have this kind of objectivity, preoccupied as I was with my adventure.

I went to the bathroom and cleaned myself up. Then read

some Anne Tyler while waiting to go down for breakfast. I planned to snag Aurelio and try to see if I could implement my plans to find out more about my principal suspects.

I still had a good hour or so before breakfast would start. I read a bit. But it was difficult to concentrate. Tried to close my eyes. But I couldn't sleep. Too many melodies running through my mind, like a storeful of radios tuned to different stations.

After showering and shaving I moisturized my burnt skin. Then went down to the pool to wait for Aurelio. It was still cool. The sun hadn't risen over the back fence yet. I stared at the pool and considered the new possibilities that had materialized after Edward had demonstrated the pool's particular nighttime deception.

With the moon and stars shining high above, the pool lights darting below the surface and the deck lamps casting a pale yellow glow, the pool—its water still—looked empty. Therefore, several possibilities bloomed in my mind: That the pool had been empty but Walter thought it was full so he dived in; accident. Or that he knew the pool was empty and wanted to kill himself; suicide. But the ones that were really prominent in my mind both involved foul play: That he was either pushed or deceived into thinking it was full; murder.

The accident theory was the least convincing. Most likely, someone had intentionally emptied the pool. I made a mental note to speak to Pearl about this.

The suicide theory was also a bit weak. I'd read nothing in Walter's journal that pointed toward suicide. Besides, there were easier ways of doing it.

I was convinced that this was a case of murder. But I'd keep the other possibilities in mind just to be safe.

The morning routine of Captain's House began, as usual, around nine o'clock. First Janis appeared and started the coffee maker which I'd forgotten about, so absorbed was I in my thoughts. Pearl came out and began breakfast. Aurelio chlorinated the pool.

We ate. Not saying much. Frank joined us shortly after we'd started. When he greeted me his eyes bored through mine like drill bits. I couldn't tell what was on his mind, but didn't really care either. I waited until Aurelio began cleaning the rooms. Then I went upstairs and began to implement my plan.

In the top drawer of the bureau in my room were several short, thick candles—in case of a power shortage due to a hurricane. I took one of the candles, and with my nail file, cut off a chunk about the size and shape of a matchbook. Kneading it with my fingers and palms, it softened. I poked my head into the hall. Aurelio was cleaning Edward's room. I went up the stairs with the wax hidden in my palm. Aurelio's key chain hung from the lock of Edward's door. Entering quietly, I made sure Aurelio had his back to me. I pulled the key, ever so gently from the lock, pressed it into the wax, slipped the impression into my pocket. Then I dropped the keys on the floor. Intentionally. No way I could have gotten them back in without jangling. Aurelio turned from the bed.

"Oops. Sorry," I said, bending to retrieve the keys. I held them out to him. "I accidentally brushed against them. Just wanted to ask when you'd be doing my room?"

He looked at me with coltish eyes. Took the keys. "Anytime you like."

"After you're through with this one?"

"No problem."

"Thank you."

I returned to my room, called my friend Allen in New York. Told him I was in Key West. "What can I do for you?" he asked.

"I need a favor, and just to remind you that you once told me you owed me one, I'll just say two words: Peggy Lee." I'd managed to introduce him to her at a cabaret several years earlier.

"Okay. I'll do anything. What do you need?"

"In a while, I'll let you know when, I want you to call this number," I gave him the downstairs number, "and ask for Aurelio."

"Who?"

"A-u-r-e-l-i-o."

"Got it."

"Just try to keep him on the phone for a couple of minutes."

"Why?"

"Can't tell you now."

"Okay."

"This makes us even."

"Right."

"I'll call you later and tell you when to call."

"Got it."

"Bye."

A short while later, Aurelio arrived to do my room. It took him about half an hour. I sat in the armchair and read Anne Tyler. We attempted to pretend that we weren't aware of each other but I kept an eye on him as I'm sure he kept an eye on me.

When he finished I waited several minutes. Then stuck my head out the door. He was doing Skip's room. Perfect. I called Allen and told him to make the call.

Less than a minute later, I heard Janis, "AURELIO! TELEPHONE!"

He ran down the stairs.

I tiptoed to Skip's room, which Aurelio had left open. Making sure no one was watching, I slipped inside.

Figuring I had less than two minutes, I quickly went to the bureau, opened drawers, shoved my hands in, feeling for something—anything—that might be concealed. In the bureau I found nothing but clothes and a baggie of grass. The closet—suitcases, shirts, pants—nothing else. I forced my hands between the box spring and the mattress, and couldn't feel anything suspicious. Then I heard a sound I couldn't identify. My blood turned into cold gazpacho as I waited to see if it would repeat. Silence—except the sound of water splashing in the pool. I looked in the drawer of the night table; some dirty underwear which I didn't bother to sniff and a small amber vial of something. I opened it, moistened the tip of my finger and brought some to my tongue; cocaine. I glanced about the room. I'd looked everywhere except inside the light fixture in the ceiling. Then I remembered: his gym bag. Beneath the bed. I dove for it and felt around inside. A Walkman, some T-shirts, a jockstrap and some suntan lotion. Nothing else. I stuck my head into the hall, darted back to my room. As my door closed and the lock clicked, I heard Aurelio bounding up the stairs.

Short of breath, my head swirling from lack of sleep, I sat

down to gather my strength. It wasn't quite noon yet. I picked up the local directory, found the number of the police station and dialed.

"Police."

"Hello. May I speak to Officer Simon, please?"

"He's not here right now, may I take a message?"

"No, thank you."

I left the house and headed for Duval Street. If I just wandered around for a while, I knew I'd run into Simon and Griffith. And, as I suspected, I found them, walking down Fleming Street. I followed. They were meandering aimlessly, occasionally hassling a street person or a kid with a loud radio.

It was getting very hot. I felt like a dishrag. A hazy glow had settled on everything, like Vaseline on a camera lens. Finally, Griffith stepped into a drug store. Simon stood at the entrance in the shade. I approached him. He looked startled when he saw me.

"I have to talk to you," I said.

"Oh?"

"It's important. About Walter Burgess's murder. Can you meet me at the alley tonight?"

"What time?"

"Midnight?"

"I'll be there."

Griffith came out.

"Good day, Officer Griffith," I said, all ebullience and charm.

He touched his nightstick to his visor.

Heading back toward the house, I turned onto Caroline Street, my heart clawing its way up my throat when I saw Joyce and Regina walking ahead of me. I slowed my pace and followed. When they got to Captain's House, they stood across the street. I approached them.

"Good afternoon, ladies. Hot enough for you?"

"Hello," they said.

"This heat's killing me," Regina added.

Joyce nodded. "Whew!"

"It seems to me," I said, pouring on all the cool charm I could summon, "that you ladies are very interested in this guest house. Would it be too presumptuous of me to invite

70

you in and give you the grand tour?" I don't know where my courage, or was it stupidity, came from.

Joyce looked horrified for a second, as though I'd uncovered her most cherished secret, but Regina quickly cooed, "Would you? That would be so kind. We've heard how beautiful it is and we're just dying to see the inside."

"Follow me."

I opened the gate, then the door and held it for them. Led them down the hall, through the living room and out to the pool. No one else was around.

"Lovely," said Joyce.

"Lovely," said Regina.

We stepped back inside and they followed me up the stairs. We entered my room and I bade them to sit on the bed. I sat on the chair. Then rose to close the door. I sat again.

"Would you like something to drink?"

"Water would be wonderful," said Regina.

"Water," Joyce agreed.

I filled two tall glasses with ice and water.

"Thank you," they said.

Someone at sometime had to tell Joyce that her husband was dead. The time had come and I had been chosen. "I suppose you haven't been reading the local paper, have you?"

"No," said Joyce, her curiosity rising.

"I think you'd better take a look at this."

I pulled out the copy of the *Ledger* I'd saved, opened it to the page with the story about Walter's death. She looked at it while Regina read over her shoulder.

Joyce looked at me. I could see her eyes turning red and watery.

I quietly asked, "Have you been in touch with him?"

She was crying now. "No." She shook her head. "No one knows I'm here."

"You followed Walter here without his knowledge so you could spy on him?"

She nodded.

"You thought he was cheating on you?"

"Yes."

Regina had her arms around Joyce's shoulders.

"I'm sorry to be the one having to ask you these questions, but I have to get some answers. Do you know who would want to kill Walter?"

Joyce looked at me, completely confused. "No."

As my heart pounded like an engine, I held onto the armrest of the chair as though my breathing depended on it.

I don't know what made me so bold, but I said, "Joyce, did you know Walter was pretending to be gay?"

She looked at me, then lost whatever hold she'd had on herself. Bawling wildly, she blurted, "Someone told me he was sometimes with men but I couldn't believe it. I had to come here to see for myself."

I got some Kleenex tissues and handed them to her.

"Joyce. He wasn't gay. Not even bi. He was just pretending, for business reasons."

"How do you know?"

"Read this."

I handed her the notebook, knowing it might cause her pain, but believing that she had to find out the truth some time and it would be best expressed in his own words. She took it from me. For several moments we stared at the walls. Then Regina cleared her throat. Joyce finished her water. We nodded at each other. They left, no more words passing between us.

I felt tired. Resting my head on my pillow, I wondered if I'd done the right thing.

NINE

I awoke sometime later. The late afternoon shadows made my room look like a still from an old black and white movie. The contrasts, the thousand shades of gray. It was classical. And campy.

My brain felt like putty and my mouth tasted like cardboard. I needed something to eat. After showering and shaving, I went to the bodega down the street. Picked up a baloney and brie sandwich, a couple of Cokes and Twinkies. On the way up to my room I heard the sounds of pots clanging in the kitchen. Curious, I went to see who was there.

Pearl stood at the sink, scouring, rinsing, drying.

"Hi!"

I must have startled her. She turned quickly, poised to smack me with a skillet, then dropped it into the soapy water. She sighed.

"Sorry," I said.

"I'm getting too old for surprises. Next time warn me or I might raise some bumps on your head." She chuckled. "I hope you're enjoying your stay."

"Oh, I am," I assured her. "Everything is wonderful. Um, Pearl, I was wondering about something."

"What's that?"

"How complicated is it to drain the pool?"

"Drain the pool...Oh, it's not complicated at all. *Filling* it is the real headache."

"So, how is it done?"

"There's two ways. We can call the pump truck and have

73

it siphoned out."

"Which I suppose is a noisy, bothersome task," I said, "which couldn't be done with any subtlety."

She nodded.

"Or?"

"Just open the drain and it all runs through underground pipes out to the ocean."

"You just have to turn a knob or a faucet?"

"That's right. Just like emptying a bathtub."

"Where is it? The knob?"

She looked at me obliquely, sort of scowling. "Over by the filtering system."

"Where's the filtering system?"

"In the far left corner."

"How often do you drain the pool?"

"Why all the questions?"

"You don't do it every night, do you?"

"The interrogation is over."

"I'm sorry," I said, "I just can't seem to get Walter Burgess off my mind. I'm still trying to figure out how it happened and why."

"Forget about it," she snapped. "It was just one of those things. The sooner we all put it behind us the better we'll be." She glared at me, her eyes like bayonets.

I went up to my room. As I ate I couldn't stop wondering if Pearl had anything to do with it, or if she was simply trying to avoid any potentially damaging publicity. Perhaps, I told myself, she was upset by the matter, maybe squeamish by nature, and didn't like thinking about it. Still, her manner was unnecessarily harsh, I thought. And realized that I knew very little about her and would not exclude her from my investigation.

I finished eating and still had time. So I went over to Woody's and sat at the bar.

I felt very self-conscious; as though being watched. But there was no one around whom I knew. All strangers to me. There was a cute number behind the bar who chatted incessantly as he deftly mixed exotic concoctions. And a big, muscular hunk playing pool, whose biceps made me shudder.

The songs on the jukebox were all familiar to me: Pointer

74

Sisters, Everly Brothers, The Sylvers, The Judds, Heart, The Beach Boys, Jackson Five. I guess it was family night.

A man about my age approached me. He didn't look overtly handsome or sexy, but was pleasant enough. And when he spoke to me I could tell immediately that he was intelligent and personable. But I was unable to take him up on his offer to leave with him. I had a date with Officer Simon in less than half an hour. Some other time, I told him, and couldn't help but wonder why it is that whenever I'm desperate no one is interested, and when the other guy is desperate I can't do it. Strange how often these things don't work.

I finished my drink and watched as the poolstick-wielding hunk bent over the table to sink the eight ball. When the seam of his jeans disappeared into the declivity of his meaty ass I realized I'd better get out while I was able.

It was dry and balmy, comparatively dry. The stars overhead made the sky look like a plugged-in canopy. In the alley where I waited it was so quiet you could hear the palm fronds massaging each other in time with the breezes. About ten minutes after midnight, Officer Simon strolled into the alley as though he owned it. Tight jeans, hightop sneakers, red tanktop—he looked great; casual, masculine, in control, sure of what he wants, secure that he'll get it.

"Good evening," I said quietly.

"Good evening."

We stood there and stared at each other for a moment. I was certain he thought I'd drop to my knees to pump him dry. But that was the last thing on my mind. I was to dominate this performance. To my way of thinking, as much as I'd enjoyed our previous encounter, until it was reciprocated, he owed me. As long as the favor was withheld, I was in charge.

"I need you to do something."

He sort of grinned, as though he knew what was coming. "Oh. What's that?"

I reached into my pocket and took out the wax impression I'd made. "I need this copied. Quietly. No questions."

He turned it over in his hands and squinted down at it. "What lock does it open?"

"I said no questions."

75

He looked at me as though I'd asked him to come out of the closet on the David Letterman show. "You can't expect me to assist you in any criminal activity."

"You don't have to know anything about this. Okay? I'll never tell anyone how I got in if I'm caught."

"Why don't you just have the key made at the hardware store?"

"It would arouse suspicion. They'd probably call the police."

"You're paranoid," he said.

Looking back, I realize he was right. I was so used to being in a big city, I thought my every move would be questioned in a small town. "Maybe. Maybe not."

"If I do it," he scratched his head as though in deep thought, "I'll have to justify it somehow."

"Look. I'm investigating the murder of Walter Burgess. Since you guys gave up on it. If I can get into Edward Mallinson's room and look around, I might be able to figure out the culprit and motive."

Simon grinned. "You should leave the police work to the police."

"But you guys aren't doing anything."

"There was no evidence to go on."

"You have to look for evidence."

He grinned again. Very handsome. But I wasn't going to let that get in my way. He placed his hands on my shoulders. And got a far-away look in his eyes. He leaned forward. I pulled back as his lips kissed the air.

"Don't try to change the subject," I said.

He looked embarrassed. "The budget for full-scale investigations in this town is pretty small."

"Will you help me or not?"

"You trying to blackmail me?"

"No. I just want your help. If you don't help me I won't hold it against you. But I'll probably never suck your cock again."

He laughed. "All right. I'll help. But forget about this wax stuff. I can jimmy the lock."

"But I can't."

"I'll do it," he said.

"But if anyone sees you at the house with me it will look

76

odd."

"So, we'll make sure no one sees me."

I thought about it for a minute. I couldn't think of a single objection. "Now might be a good time," I said. "He's probably at the disco and he'll probably stay there until it closes."

"Let's go."

I followed him out of the alley and we walked to Captain's House. A mounting sense of fear enveloped my being. I was aware that I was suddenly doing things that were potentially dangerous. Possibly even lethal. And I was always the kind who avoided any kind of complication or risky situation. How did I know I could trust this cop? What would happen if we were caught? Part of me wanted to flee from the whole affair, but another part of me was drawn to the guts of it for reasons I can't figure out. It was more than boredom or curiosity. Not simply the sense of wanting to right a wrong or bring justice to a criminal enterprise. I don't know if I was being driven by something within me, or pulled by something from without. I only know I continued in the direction that, then and now, seemed inevitable.

Officer Simon assumed control of our unit as soon as we reached our destination. After I unlocked the gate and we were in the front yard, he hid in the azalea bushes while I opened the front door. As instructed, I walked to the back of the house and looked out at the pool. There was no one in the backyard, living room or kitchen. The house was so still you could hear the whirring of the ceiling fans. I ran upstairs and unlocked my room. Then went back down and stuck my head out the front door. I signaled Simon and he moved quickly, silently up the stairs and into my room. When the door closed behind him, I went up to the third floor, stood on the landing and listened. I could hear snoring sounds coming from the Japanese guys' room. Tiptoeing to Edward's door, I knocked gently, then placed my ear against the wood. I knocked again. Nothing. I quickly crept down the stairs. I nodded to Simon, we went up. After withdrawing a metallic something-or-other from his pocket, he stuck it in the keyhole and wriggled it around. He pushed it in further, withdrew it slightly, twisted until it caught. Then he turned it smoothly until we heard a click. He looked up at me and grinned. Pleased with himself. I could feel his body heat. I tried to think about other things. He pushed the door open and walked in. Looked around. Beckoned me to enter. Then he closed the door and I switched on the light. We hadn't discussed what was to be done at this stage, but instinctively, he started going through the drawers of the bureau as I ransacked first the closet, then the chifforobe. The difficult part was that we didn't know what we were looking for. I hoped to find a diary, journal or notebook, letters, appointment book, address and phone directory. I had no idea what Simon was searching for. We went through shoes, socks, pants, shirts, underwear, toilet articles, towels, blankets, sheets, pillowcases. I hauled a suitcase from the closet and—in a side pocket—found a combination appointment book with address and phone numbers. I turned to the B section to look up Burgess. It was listed! As I was about to skim the calendar to see if there were any meetings with him, or mentions, we heard a sound in the hall. Two voices. Moving as quickly and as silently as an arrow, Simon closed the drawers, turned off the light and stepped into the chifforobe. He indicated that I should follow, so I stumbled in behind him. We sat facing one another with our knees to our chins, among dangling shirts, slacks and jackets. Wedging the tips of his fingers into the slats of the louvered doors, he pulled them closed. A moment later the door to the room opened and the light went on. Horizontal shafts of light tumbled through the slats of the chifforobe. I pushed a pant leg aside and peered out. Edward had brought someone home. Most likely for the night. And Simon and I were stuck in a tiny, cramped, almost airless space, forced to remain silent and unobtrusive, unable to ingest, expectorate or evacuate.

I tried to see who the other person was. But all I could discern was a pair of jean-clad legs and white running shoes. The man beneath the clothing could have been anywhere between eighteen and forty-five. No matter how much I strained my neck to look through a higher slat, all I could see was the lower body. So I cocked my ears and listened carefully to every word and inflection to see if I could recognize the voice.

"Nice room."

"Best house in Key West," said Edward.

78

"So they say."

"Please sit," said Edward.

I heard the bed creak. The refrigerator opened, pop-tops whooshed, liquid gurgled against glass. I saw Edward lurch toward the bed. They were both probably a little drunk.

"So what brings you to Key West besides the sun and sex? You said something earlier about being down on business." His voice was nondescript, lacking any distinctive characteristics. Not too high or low, unusually raspy or smooth. He didn't talk fast or slow, his accent was General American.

"Trying to get a few minor things accomplished. Scouting locations for a new business, aside from the R and R."

"Here, let me do that."

I heard the sounds of zippers. Shoes thudded to the floor. Belt buckles clicked.

The light switched off. The chifforobe was dark. I could feel the warmth of Simon's breath. He shifted his feet slightly and jabbed my butt. It was getting so hot my shirt stuck to the sweat on my back and chest. There was gabardine pressing against my cheek. I had to sneeze but managed to squelch it. The air was getting stale and I felt drowsy. My butt ached where it connected with hard wood and my legs got numb.

As I wondered if Simon was as uncomfortable, I heard the susurration of kissing. Sucky, slurpy sounds. The bedsprings creaked with the horizontal choreography of two adult male bodies. I wished I was on that bed with Simon. Or Edward.

Hoping that the sounds they were making would provide protection, I risked breathing deeply and tried to clear my head. Then Simon took a chance that the thrashing sounds would camouflage a hushed voice. "How are you doing?" he whispered.

"Okay. You?"

"Fine."

Part of me wanted to explode with laughter. There we were, crouched in the dark, concealed in antique furniture, with two guys indulging in sexual gymnastics not more than five feet away. It was funny. No denying. But part of me was terrified. What if we were discovered? What would the penalty be? Could Officer Simon be de-badged if he was caught doing something like this? Could I be sued? I was certain we'd broken laws, wondered if we could be arrested, wanted to ask him about the risks we were taking but decided that conversation would have to wait.

I heard the sound of lubrication on skin. Then the splat of smooth flesh on smooth flesh.

"Ouch," said the stranger.

"Sorry," said Edward.

Then the sound of a broad naked back against taut linen.

I could hear Simon chuckling beneath his breath. Then I felt a belch erupting in my stomach. Fortunately I learned how to burp silently years ago.

Eventually the rhythmic pattern of moans, groans and creaks permeated the room. The tempo increased as did the frequency and volume of the oral ejaculations. Finally, one of them cried out in ecstasy. The sounds of two men fucking ceased. And shortly thereafter, we could hear the cacophonous polyphony of two snoring sleepers.

"I gotta pee," Simon whispered.

"Me too."

"We gotta get outa here."

I thought about it for a moment. "Don't you think we should wait until they wake up and leave?"

"No! That could take all night if they're stoned or drunk enough. Besides, what if they wake up and decide to look in here?"

"You're right."

"Just be quiet," he said, "it'll probably take disco speakers to wake them up."

Holding our breaths, as delicately and as cautiously as we were able, we opened the chifforobe doors and got out, then crept across the room. I stumbled over a shoe, but caught myself before any noise could be heard. Freezing into a statue, I listened to see if I'd disturbed either slumber-slug. They continued to ignore us.

Simon got to the door and carefully turned the knob. It clicked as it opened. Sounded like a cannon to me. We got into the hall, closed the door and rose to our feet. I felt cramped and achy all over. Suddenly, I heard footsteps coming up the stairs. Simon grabbed my arm. I leaned over the banister, couldn't tell who it was, but I could see that he or she was coming up the first staircase. I pulled Simon along behind me. We scurried down the upper staircase and disappeared into my room just as whoever it was reached the landing. If we hadn't left my door unlocked and I'd had to fumble with the key, we would have been caught.

The first thing I did was search my room to see if anything had been taken or tampered with during the time we were upstairs. Nothing was amiss. Then I realized that a locked door hadn't prevented anyone from entering previously.

I wanted to get Simon out of my room and back on the street. It was almost dawn. First, he used the bathroom. Then it was my turn. What a relief! Simon appeared to be pleased as well. He sat on the bed, yawned a couple of times. I went to the door and peered out into the hall. With all of the stealth and discretion I could muster, I left the room, closed the door and went downstairs.

Aurelio was cleaning the walls in the hallway.

"Good morning," I said.

"Oh, hi," he said, startled. He hadn't expected anyone to be up so early.

"Looks like it's going to be a beautiful day," I said.

"Yes," he agreed.

I had to justify this unusually early appearance. "I guess a dip will wake me up," I said, as though I'd been planning one.

I went out to the pool. Stripped. Dove in, swam to the far end and back. The water was chilly. I shivered as I went, naked, from the pool to the towel hamper. After a quick rubdown, I tied the towel around my waist, grabbed my clothing and went back inside. Passing Aurelio I said, "Bracing, refreshing."

He smiled.

I went up to the room.

"Aurelio, the houseboy, is washing the walls in the front hallway."

"And in a little while everyone will be up and about. Looks like I'm camping out for a while," he said and stretched out on the bed.

"Why?"

"Because I can't be seen leaving here in my civvies. That's why."

81

And then I saw the light. "Because it could be inferred that you spent the night here with someone, i.e. another man, and then people might think that you're queer and heavens! the world would just stop turning, wouldn't it?"

"Cut the shit!" he said, looking like he wanted to throttle me. "If the people of this town knew I was, you know, I'd be out of a job."

"Maybe. Maybe not."

"That's easy for you to say, coming from a big city. Things are different here."

"Do you like sneaking around and pretending to be something that you're not?"

"No, I don't like it. But I live with it."

"Fine," I said. But I was angry. I wanted him to proclaim his identity to the world. I was really getting incensed with all of the subterfuge, the lying, the deceit that seemed to touch everything and everyone I could see.

Just then the telephone rang.

Without thinking about it or asking if he should, Simon picked it up. "Hello? Hold on a second." He held the receiver out to me. "It's for you."

"That's what I figured," I said, trying to conceal the sarcasm. "Hello?"

"You little shit!"

"Paul?"

"There's only one reason why you'd have another man in your room at this hour of the morning. If you had half a brain you would at least have answered the phone yourself and tried not to flaunt your lies, evasions, deceptions."

"Paul, I can explain!"

But he didn't give me a chance. He slammed the receiver down. I felt like pure slime as I followed suit.

"Thanks a lot," I said to Simon, the sarcasm underlined, bold, italics.

"I gotta make a call," he said, offering no apology or anything else.

He phoned his station and told the desk sergeant he wasn't well and wouldn't be in.

Then to me, he said, "I guess we should get some sleep."

"Great idea."

He stripped down to nothing. I tried to look away. But his

body was like a magnet and my eyes were like iron filings. I pulled back the bedspread and we got in. There may as well have been a partition down the middle of the bed. He stayed as close to his edge as he could, and I did the same. He was sleeping soundly moments later.

I lay there thinking as the room lightened up with the morning sun. As tired as my body was, my brain felt hyperactive. But it wasn't the case of Walter Burgess that played tag with my synapses. I thought about myself and sex and love. And wondered why, at the age of thirty-four, I was so confused.

I listed the contradictory facts.

I was in love with Paul, yet ever since I'd arrived in Key West, I'd been searching for sex.

I was very attracted to Simon, but at the same time, I hated the power his sexiness held over me.

If I loved Paul, why was I attracted to Simon?

Why didn't my revulsion for Simon's personality override my desire for his body?

I'm not naive enough to think that sex equals love and love equals sex. I learned all about that misconception years ago. When I was just a silly lad I believed that you had sex with the person you loved, or loved the person you had sex with, except for those infrequent occasions when one partner had a little action on the side. This was a very simple concept for a child like myself to grasp.

But growing older and experiencing these things for oneself was an entirely different matter from contemplating them in the abstract. My love for Paul, I now realized, had very little if anything to do with his physical presence. It was his intelligence, his warmth, his generosity that had brought us together. Sure, we had great sex when we'd first met. Now the great sex was rare. But the intelligence, warmth and generosity were still abundantly evident (except when we fought which was not too often).

When sex with Paul had become less incendiary, less frequent, my desires and cravings did not diminish. I guess I'd assumed that the cooling off of our sexual encounters somehow mirrored a change in our other relations. But what I was beginning to understand was that domesticity and monogamy do not necessarily diminish one's need for

83

variety, experimentation, occasional risk-taking.

What I wanted was the security of living with Paul, but the freedom to indulge in outside affairs. Which, at first, I thought was a part of my nature as a gay man. I'd been rather promiscuous before meeting Paul. After six years of living together I again wanted to be promiscuous without upsetting the peaceful domestic arrangement I'd searched for. And now I realized that it wasn't my gayness that offered the temptation. It was simply my maleness. Men—regardless of whether they like to suck cock or screw pussy—like to fool around. Sex is fun. Sex is power. Sex is the gold star you get for showing up at work on time, paying your bills, opening doors, saying please and thank you.

I guess the confusion resulted from guilt. I wanted to stay with Paul, but only on my terms. And Simon had thrown all of those terms into question. I despised him but I wouldn't be satisfied until I'd gotten everything from him that I wanted. Which, should I succeed, would estrange me from Paul, which would destroy everything I'd worked so hard to create.

As soon as Simon was out of my bed and out of the house, I'd try to keep him out of my life.

TEN

I'm in a coffin with Simon. Underwater. We're fucking in this tiny space as water leaks in. It's getting harder to breathe. Suddenly the top of the coffin snaps off, the water rushes in, and we're floating in a thick green soup with seaweed, coral and sharp-toothed barracudas. All around float corpses, wide-eyed, droopy-tongued, stiff-limbed. I try to swim away but my feet are tangled in spiky tendrils of kelp. I feel myself fighting to breathe and escape, trying to get to the surface. Just as I feel like I will implode, I wake up.

I heard a knocking at the door. And struggled to grasp what was happening. Then, more knocking, and "It's Aurelio. Do you want your room done up now?"

"Not today," I said groggily.

"Okay."

Simon was snoring. He hadn't stirred. The clock said 12:38. I lay there, thinking. Simon's words ricocheted in my mind. His defense of the closet. Were his fears justified or was he just a coward? Sure, there's potentially dangerous consequences if you happen to be gay and are honest about it. But there are dangers too in concealing who you are. Blackmail, for one. And then the irony hit me like a guided missile: Walter had pretended to be gay. And he was dead. Simon was pretending to be straight. What would his fate be? Most likely, dismissal from his job if he ever gets caught with his pants down in the wrong alley with the wrong dude. If nothing else, should the truth ever be made known, who would trust him?

The sooner I could get Simon out of my room and back on the street, I could resume my investigation. I had a new clue: Walter's address and phone number in Edward's directory.

And I wanted to talk to Frank. See if what I'd found out from Skip had any bearing on what he would have to say.

So I got into some clothes and left the room. Simon hadn't budged or deviated from his sleeper's rhythm. I went downstairs and found Frank floating in the center of the pool.

"Hi!" I greeted him. "I was hoping I'd find you."

"Oh, really?" he said, with a tone that implied, prove it.

"I was wondering if we could have a talk?"

"Sure."

"Someplace private," I added.

"Your room?"

"Um, no, it's really a mess, how about yours?"

"Okay," he said and crawled out of the pool. I followed him to his room. He closed and locked the door.

The afternoon sun through the slightly parted Venetian blinds striped the room with swirling motes. It gave the four-poster bed, the paisley bedspread and the armoire the look of a daguerreotype.

I sat on the bed. He sat right beside me, our thighs touching. I got up and sat in the big easy chair.

Frank played with the alligator applique on his shirt. "What's the scoop?" he asked and I wondered if that was a natural expression of his or if he was mocking me and my career.

"I'll get right to the point. This concerns Walter Burgess."

"Oh, so we're talking about old news."

"There have been some new developments," I explained.

"And you're still playing Shirley, I mean, Sherlock Holmes."

I ignored the remark. "Did you know Walter was straight? That Skip was pretending to be his boyfriend?"

"I don't know anything about it." I couldn't tell if the look on his face was one of anger, or if that was his natural expression.

"When you saw Walter did it seem like he was just pretending, what I mean is, was there anything unusual about him?"

86

His face scrunched up like a peach pit. "If you persist with these questions and accusations you could get into all kinds of trouble."

"Like what?"

"Lawsuits. Invasion of privacy. Defamation of character. Harassment."

I didn't know if he was bluffing or not. And I wasn't taking any chances. "Sorry to bother you," I said with as much deference as I could.

He rose and opened the door. "If you have any more questions you can direct them to my lawyer."

"I'll remember that," I said.

Walking to my room I heard the door slam behind me. I placed Frank at the top of my mental list of suspects. His response to my questions, I was convinced, was not that of an innocent man. I was certain he knew a lot more than he was willing to tell.

I entered my room. Simon was still sleeping. I decided to wake him up.

By this time I was very angry with him. I'd managed to convince myself that if he'd simply had a key made for me, instead of insisting on taking control, we might not have gotten stuck in the chifforobe.

I started out quietly, gently.

"Simon...time to get up."

He didn't stir.

"Simon," louder, "it's time to wake up."

He didn't budge.

"Simon," louder still, "if you don't wake up in three seconds I'm going to douse you with toxic waste."

Nothing.

I got a glass of water and threw it at his face. He woke up.

"What happened?" he asked, fearful.

"Nothing. Just a little water. Are you always this difficult to get up?"

"Huh?"

"You're a pretty deep sleeper."

"So I've been told. What time is it?"

"Almost three."

"I'm hungry."

I was too. "Unless you're brave enough to leave right now,

87

you're stuck for another seven or eight hours."

He didn't like it when I implied that he was cowardly.

"Got anything in the fridge?"

"Just soda and beer."

"We could call Gino's for a pizza. They deliver."

"Fine," I said.

Then we argued over peppers, onions, extra cheese, mushrooms, ground beef. Not surprisingly, neither wanted anchovies (I've never met anyone who has).

While I straightened up the room a little, Simon used the bathroom.

He emerged, dripping wet, naked, and I had to cross my legs to disguise my response. Then he stretched out on the bed like an odalisque. I couldn't help but try to gain some advantage over his sexual power. He asked, "You're a writer, you said?"

"Music critic."

When he inquired further I piled up the bullshit like a tractor.

"Is it fun?" he asked.

"Oh, loads," I said. "Especially when you hear about the real insider secret stuff."

"Like what?" he asked eagerly, like a seal waiting for the fish to be tossed.

"Well, you've heard of Barbra Streisand," I said.

"Of course," he said, as though praying, "I adore her."

And your favorite song is "Send In The Clowns," I said to myself.

"And my favorite song is 'Send In The Clowns'."

"Oh!" I said, feigning surprise, "then you've heard of Stephen Sondheim?"

"He's a genius."

"Yes," I said, "he is. You know the Streisand *Broadway Album?*"

"I wish she'd recorded it on that album," he gushed.

"Don't we all," I said. "Anyway, just between you and me," I lowered my voice for effect, he scrunched up his shoulders and listened breathlessly, "when they were working on the album Sister Babs treated Brother Stevie like shit, to the point where he started referring to her as the Cuntess—"

"The *Cunt*ess?"

"—that's right, and then, by accident, one of his assistants called her that *right to her face!* She almost killed the guy."

Simon's jaw was about to unhinge. He'd swallowed my lie like a snake eats frogs. "No shit! Wow! And you find out about this kind of stuff all the time?"

"All the time," I said, rather pleased with myself.

A few moments later the pizza arrived. Aurelio came to the room to fetch me. Simon hid in the closet and I pretended I was alone. I went down, paid the delivery man, then returned to the room.

Simon emerged. We ate in silence. The room darkened as the sun began to fall.

After eating, Simon leaned back and burped. Then he said, "We have some time to kill. Tell me all about this murder case you seem to have all the answers to." His sarcasm was undisguised.

For a moment my stomach felt like it had been microwaved. When the wave of nausea passed, I took a long breath, glued my eyes to the pupil's of Simon's, and made the most persuasive sales pitch I could.

"You may recall the sight of Walter Burgess's body—what remained of it—splattered all over the bottom of that pool. The red and pink on black was pretty unforgettable, I think." My jaw was set, my mouth hard, my eyes unrelenting. I dared him to mock me. He betrayed no emotion. "I was quite prepared to try my best to forget all about it, stupidly thinking that the cops—you guys—would do something." I waited to see if he would agree that I'd been stupid. He remained indifferent. "We come now to the all important question—why *should* anything be done? Well, the answer is a) Walter was a human being, b) murder is against the law, and c) whoever killed him could kill again. Stop me when your brain says *tilt*." He continued to play his mannequin game. "Now here's where it gets interesting. In talking to Frank Fiore, I caught Skip Dunnock in a lie. Or so I thought. That got me suspicious because Skip claimed that he didn't know Walter and Frank claimed he, Skip, did. I subsequently found out that Skip *did* know Walter, but anyway, that's what got me started. Then, someone stole Walter's journal from me, which Skip had loaned me, and then it was returned. By person or persons unknown. When

I finally got around to reading it there was information indicating that Walter was being blackmailed. Apparently, he was really straight and pretending to be gay. Something that you, Simon, should be able to understand." He was as inanimate as a doorknob. "Perhaps I've read too many Raymond Chandler's and Dash Hammett's but if I'm not mistaken, I believe that blackmail and murder go together like love and marriage, horse and carriage. Are you with me, Simon?" He nodded. I continued. "Then I found out that Walter's wife is here in Key West, and she was here while he was still alive and he didn't know it. And, bear with me now, then someone pushed me into the pool and told me to go home and stop poking around. Granted, getting soaked is not a criminal offense, but clearly, I was threatened. And last, but certainly not least, I found an interesting tidbit earlier—just before you and I were forced to hide."

"Oh? What's that?"

"Edward also claimed that he didn't know Walter, but his address book proves it a lie."

Simon yawned and stretched. "Fascinating," he said. "You think it's safe to leave yet?"

His lack of interest infuriated me. I decided I'd protect him from his impersonation no longer. "Gee," I said innocently, "let's check." I motioned with my finger for him to follow me to the door. He slipped into his clothes as I opened it. Then I whispered, "Most of the guests are most likely eating dinner or napping. The house people are probably resting. Now's probably as good a time as any." I stuck my head out the door. "Sounds pretty quiet, looks pretty clear," I said, "check it out."

Simon leaned out into the hall.

"Can you hear anything from downstairs?" I whispered.

"No," he said, and took a tentative step out into the hall. I pushed him clear of the door, slammed it shut, and locked it.

Simon knocked once. Quietly. I ignored him. He couldn't very well start pounding and yelling—not if he wanted to get away unnoticed.

I pictured him tiptoeing down the stairs and out the front door. If he got caught that was his problem. I was tired of babysitting. And tired of his attitude. If the world found out he was gay that wouldn't bother me anymore than a flea sneezing in China.

I sat there for a minute. Tried to think of what I should do next. But the decision was made without any input from me. The telephone rang.

ELEVEN

I picked up the receiver, expecting to have another fight with Paul. But, surprise, it was someone I hadn't planned on hearing from.

"This is Regina Carson, Joyce Burgess's friend?"

"Hello, what can I do for you?"

"I've got to see you right away."

"Me?"

"Yes."

"Why?"

"I can't say over the phone."

I told her to come to Captain's House.

My room needed straightening up. I bundled the leftover pizza crusts with the greasy box and brought the mess downstairs to the kitchen where I deposited it in the trash compactor.

No one was around. Simon had probably escaped unobserved. I returned to my room. And had nothing to do but think. Which usually leads to problems.

I wanted to go home. I'd had enough of Key West and Walter Burgess. I missed the familiarity and comfort waiting for me in New York. I missed Paul.

Then I heard the bell and hastened down to answer the door. Regina greeted me nervously. I led her up to my room.

Her hair teased way out to there, gobs of gaudy face paint everywhere, she looked like a strawberry tart with a thyroid condition. I don't know why but I always associate this look with stupidity. It seems that every time I'm in a public situation and I overhear someone who looks like this, she invariably manages to say things that leave me impressively unimpressed. Do women do themselves up like this to lure men? I wasn't interested. Then I noticed that she'd doused herself with one of those cloyingly sweet perfumes, the odor of which tends to make me nauseous. I suggested that we go out to the veranda.

We sat on the white wicker chairs with the white wicker table between us. The gentle breeze did not budge Regina's stiff hair. I offered her a soft drink which she accepted. Then she stared at me with all of the gravity in her soul.

"There are some things—regarding Walter and Joyce—that I have to tell you," she said, clearly choked up. "But this is all strictly confidential. If it comes down to it, I'll deny everything."

"Slow down," I said. "Why are you telling this to me?"

"Because you seem like a nice young man—and the cops don't care at all and I desperately need to talk to someone."

"Where's Joyce?"

"She went back home. I told her I'd stay and see about the body," she had a little difficulty with this word, "and any other problems that might arise."

She spoke in a manner—intelligent and controlled—that seemed to clash with her garish appearance.

"What do you have to tell me about, or ask me?"

"This is regarding Walter."

"I thought so. Didn't think you wanted to talk to me about ancient Ethiopian philosophy," I said to try to lighten the mood.

She forced a grin. Then her face became tight and serious. "The police around here don't know what's going on, but I do."

"Really?"

"Yes. They don't know if he was murdered or what, but even greater than their ignorance is their bigotry."

"Go on."

"The thing is, they don't care. Because they think he was gay."

She paused to let me catch up but I was already there.

"I know."

"How do you know?"

"Not important. Walter was pretending to be gay but he

was really straight. I know the whole song and dance."

She looked astonished. As though I'd performed a miracle or farted or something.

"Everything?"

"I'm not sure."

"Well, these are the facts. Walter and I were having an affair. There, I've said it. The worst is over now. I know it was wrong. I've hated myself for deceiving Joyce. She's really my very best friend. But Walter and I had something special. And he was able to share with me certain things that Joyce would never have understood."

"Such as?"

"Well, his business dilemma, for example. If he hadn't gone undercover, so to speak, to expand his business, he never would have been as successful as he was. When it came time to buy his first club, Joyce was against it. But Walter knew what he was doing. So from that time on, he pretty much kept Joyce away from all of his business dealings. She never would have accepted his modus operandi of dressing like the Roman when in Rome. So he turned to me because I gave support and understanding when he could find none at home."

"If Walter knew what he was doing why is he no longer doing it?"

"He took his life because he thought Joyce found out about his secret life."

"Suicide?"

"Yes. Walter was coming here for a business trip. He told Joyce he was going to California. But she found out otherwise. So she decided to follow him, in secret, to see what he was up to. She asked me to accompany her. I agreed, thinking that I could spare them both some pain. Well, after we were here for a few days, Walter saw her and me. He contacted me through Skip—you know who he is?"

"Yes."

"And Walter and I met briefly. He thought she already knew. I told him she didn't but was very suspicious. He didn't believe me. He figured I was commiserating with her. We had quite a scene. He thought I'd betrayed him and that Joyce knew everything. But believe me, she didn't know a thing. But anyway, he committed suicide because he assumed he'd lose us both and that Joyce would drag him through an ugly, well-publicized divorce which would ruin his business."

Regina sniffed. Then drew a hanky from her purse. She dabbed her eyes and blew her nose.

"What about the blackmail angle? Isn't it possible he was murdered?"

Regina looked at me aghast. "Blackmail?"

"He didn't tell you about the blackmail, huh?"

"No," she said, astonished.

"I read all about it in his journal."

"Journal?"

"What I gave to Joyce the other day."

"Oh."

At that moment I realized that Regina didn't know as much as she thought. It occurred to me that my murder theory had as much validity as her suicide theory. So I tried to elicit more information.

"You know Skip?"

"Yes."

"Tell me about him," I said as casually as I could.

"Of course, you know, he's straight too."

"Of course?" This bit of news really fucked with my sense of equilibrium.

"Yes. You see, Walter needed a younger guy around to convince his clients and associates that he was one of them. But he was afraid of hiring a *real* hustler for two reasons: the obvious one, blackmail, and also because he was afraid that a real gay person might try to seduce him. He was really quite paranoid about sex. Except with me. But, anyway, he found Skip. The two of them acted like a couple whenever it was expedient. Skip was paid very well. Walter was able to successfully carry off his charade. Everyone was happy."

"If everyone was so happy then why is Walter dead?"

"I told you, he committed suicide because he thought Joyce had discovered his secret."

"I'm still not convinced it was suicide. Why did Walter and Skip try to create the impression—at least here at the guest house, anyway—that they didn't know each other? And why would Walter choose such a complicated, messy way to die? Why not pills or something?"

"Because he was overwhelmed with grief and not in his right mind."

I still wasn't convinced.

Complete darkness had descended over the island. The moon and stars cast lazy shadows over everything I could see. Regina and I sat in silence for several minutes. Like we'd reached an accord. She had all the answers. But I wasn't satisfied with any of them. I guess the silence became too uncomfortable, because Regina finally spoke, changing the subject.

"It's obvious you're not a detective. What do you do for a living?"

"I'm a writer."

"Are you planning to write a book about Walter?"

"I'm a music critic."

"Oh? How exciting!"

"Sometimes."

"I *love* music."

"I do too."

"What kind do you write about?"

"All kinds."

This was getting to be a very boring topic, as far as I was concerned.

"How thrilling it must be to always hear symphony orchestras in concert halls."

"Yes."

"My husband, George, says that the symphony is dead but I don't agree. All of those gorgeous scores for movies like *Star Wars* and *Close Encounters*. Those are the modern symphonies."

"You must be quite a music fan," I said.

"Well, I took piano from five to thirteen. And then I studied music appreciation. I used to sing in the church choir. Anyway, George likes to see all the new movies and a lot of times I don't like what's on the screen but I close my eyes and enjoy the music."

"Regina, where are you staying? In case I have to get in touch?"

She gave me the address and phone number.

"Since the police don't give a damn about this, I'm going to try to find the murderer—starting with Skip Dunnock."

"You will discover it's a suicide. But if I can be of any help—don't hesitate."

"How much longer will you be in town?"

"A few more days."

I walked her to my door and said goodbye. Then sat in the armchair. The talk with her about music had been interesting. Movie scores and modern symphonies. I filed it away for future mulling.

There were two things I had to do: try to get to the truth about Skip and try to find out if I could reconstruct the events that led up to the fatal moment. Perhaps if I spoke to Pearl, Janis and Aurelio I might get some insight into what had happened that night. And maybe that would lead to answers I could believe in.

I'd speak to the house folks tomorrow. Tonight I had to find Skip. I asked myself where he might be. His room? A knock on his door yielded no response. Maybe he'd drugged himself again? I wasn't about to break down his door to find out.

Woody's and Streets were the obvious alternatives.

I went to the bathroom to freshen myself, then changed my clothes. As I was about to turn off the light and lock the door, the phone rang. I recognized the voice right away.

"Don't hang up, I'm sorry," he blurted with haste.

"Paul. How are you?"

"I'm fine. Look. I'm sorry about this morning."

"Forget it."

"No, no, this is important. In the first place—you have a right to your own privacy. In the second place—I should have waited for an explanation before jumping to conclusions."

"Do you want the whole truth and nothing but?"

"Even if it kills me," he said.

"All right, here goes..." and I explained about Simon and I breaking into Edward's room, hiding in the chifforobe, the waiting in my room until he could escape without notice (I left out the part about us sleeping in the same bed, just as I'd omitted the blowjob in the rain from my earlier report) "...and finally I just couldn't stand having him in the room. I detest closeted people and moreover, I was pissed at him for picking up the phone when you called. Don't you think

97

it's improper for someone to answer someone else's phone without permission?"

"I'm sure Ann and Abby would have lots to say on that subject," he said, "but let's backtrack a second. You weren't joking about this murder thing?"

"No. It's real. A guy was killed—I saw the body, in fact, I discovered the body—and it seems I'm the only person in the entire world who is curious enough to want to find out the particulars."

"Are you in any danger?"

"Not really. Someone got into my room to steal a notebook and someone pushed me in the pool. Aside from that..."

"I think you should come home right away. Don't wait until tomorrow. Leave now."

"Tomorrow?" I asked, stunned.

"Yes! Your return flight's scheduled for tomorrow afternoon. Maybe you can get something for tonight."

"You know, I'd completely forgotten. I'm so glad you reminded me. There's no way I can leave tomorrow. I'm so close to the answers I can almost taste them. I think I'll cancel for tomorrow and try for something in a few days. By that time the mystery should be solved and I'll be eager to get home."

"You're staying? Why? Why should you give a flying fuck who killed this guy? He's a total stranger, right?"

"Right."

"And you went to Key West to relax, right?"

"Right."

"So?"

"Look, Paul, this is important to me. I want to find out _why_ this guy was killed. And who did it. If people go around killing each other and no one asks any questions—can you imagine what this world would be like?"

"Stop kidding yourself. It wouldn't be any different from the way it is right now. The world is a cesspool and all the people floating around in it are turds."

"If I agreed with you," I said, "I'd have no reason to get out of bed in the morning."

"I didn't mean it. I just think you should come home. Be on that plane tomorrow."

"Or else?"

"Or else nothing. Be on that plane!"

I hated when he tried to bully me like that. "Look, Paul, I've got to run—there's a hot murder case screaming for my attention. I'll call you soon. Bye."

I hung up. Called the airline to postpone my return. Shut off the lights, locked the door and left Captain's House. A cool breeze dried the sweat on my forehead. I walked slowly, trying to shake the sound of Paul's voice from my inner ear. But it was insistent.

It had rained earlier in the day. The streets were slick and the air had that after-the-deluge aroma. The puddles looked like quicksilver beneath the slick beams of brightness cast by the moon and the stars.

TWELVE

Duval Street was fairly deserted as I walked through the door to Woody's. It's not often that I feel the need for a drink, but on that occasion it seemed necessary. Bourbon on ice is perfect for such times. It's warm and cool at the same time, relaxes your nervous system immediately, your brain and muscles soon after.

In the few moments before I started looking around, trying to locate Skip, a scenario of Walter Burgess's life passed through my mind. Here's this guy—not bad-looking, middle-aged. Owns a bunch of successful businesses. Has a pretty wife. Sleeps with her best friend. Has a fake boyfriend to create the impression he's gay. I told myself, this must have been the most twisted guy in the universe. Why did I care who killed him? If I'd ever known him, I might not have liked him very much. But he was a human being, apparently harmless, certainly not a criminal, and he'd been murdered. Viciously. The horror of his death had burned through my eyes, branded my brain. Perhaps if I'd never seen the sight of him, mangled and splattered, I wouldn't have been so concerned. But I'd been forced to confront his brutal death and couldn't keep my mind on anything else. I was determined to go the whole route and see what lurked behind all of the locked doors, whispered words, ugly truths and painful deceptions.

The bourbon eased me into a steady, comfortable rhythm. I glanced around the bar to check out the scene. Middle of the week, not yet midnight, the population was somewhat sparse.

Beyond the pool table, in a corner, Skip stood talking to someone. They both drank beer from cans. Skip looked great as usual. Something between the captain of the junior varsity and a Manhattan actor/waiter/model. His companion was a short, dark-haired man with a moustache and glasses. They spoke with obvious intensity, their gestures rather animated.

I waited until I could intervene. Perhaps one of them would go to the bathroom or come to the bar. The jukebox was turned up louder than usual. All kinds of goodies sought the attention of my auditory canals: Whitney Houston, Flock of Seagulls, The Four Seasons, Lou Reed, Ernest Tubb, Suzanne Vega. I sang along, sotto voce, and watched the pool players.

Eventually Skip walked away from the guy he'd been talking to. He came to the bar, about ten feet away from me, and ordered another beer. When the transaction was completed I joined him. After exchanging the expected pleasantries I got right to the meat of my quest.

"I've got to talk to you, in private, at your earliest convenience."

"What about?"

"Walter."

"Oh." He didn't seem to be thrilled by the prospect.

"I found out some new information and need to corroborate with you."

"Oh, yeah? What kind of new information?"

"This really isn't the right time or place."

"If you want to talk to me you gotta tell me what it's about—unless you want to pay—in which case we can play it any way you want."

I was taken aback more than slightly.

"You mean, if I pay your usual hustler fee, you'll tell me the truth?"

"That's right," he said, as though we'd reached an agreement. But I was angry. No one had ever bartered with me over the truth before. It was kind of disquieting. But it occurred to me that in America, the truth is held in opposition to money all the time. Every time an advertiser creates a marketing campaign, every time a politician speaks in public, we allow, we accept the lies.

"Fuck you, you little twerp," I said. "You'll tell me the truth, for nothing, or I'll go to the police with the new information I've uncovered." I was bluffing, but how could he know?

If his eyes had been coals they would have been red-hot. He looked like he might strike me or bolt any second. "Later!" he said and stomped out the door.

I stood there. Debating whether to buy another drink. But before I could decide, the man who'd been talking to Skip came over and introduced himself. His name was Mark.

"That Skip, he's quite a hunkette," he said.

"Yes."

"Funny for a hustler, though," he said.

"Oh?"

"The other night I saw him at Streets—the disco."

"I know it," I said.

"So I went over and asked him to dance. He told me to put my money where my mouth is. So I handed him a fifty and asked if it was enough. He just looked at it and told me it was enough but he wasn't in the mood. Fine. I walked away. And then, I ran into him tonight and offered him a hundred if he'd come back to my room. He told me I'm not his type. Since when does a hustler turn down business?"

"You got me," I said, then nodded politely through several more moments of conversation. As soon as the statute of limitations on politeness to strangers in a bar had expired, I excused myself and left.

Skip's refusal to do business with Mark was an interesting bit of news. It either confirmed Regina's claim that he wasn't gay. Or, on the other hand, maybe he wasn't really a hustler at all. The only proof I had was hearsay and his own testimony. Could he be lying about his occupation? Maybe he was a killer for hire, or a private investigator, or just a crazy kid with a penchant for trouble.

I went to Streets to have another drink.

More bourbon on ice. It tasted even better than the first. The music was loud. Too loud for my ears. When I was younger and used to go dancing often—back in the mid-seventies—I thought the music was never loud enough. My friends and I would scream PUMP IT, hoping the volume would be turned from deafening to lethal. But nowadays no matter what the dynamic level is, it's usually far too much for me.

I saw Edward dancing with a gorgeous Hispanic guy—mocha, solid and sinewy. Watched them for a while. They moved almost as one. Then I went to the video arcade. Frank was playing a game. I managed to pass through without him noticing me. I searched every corner of the establishment looking for Skip. But he was not to be found anywhere—the cabaret, the pool room, the lavatories.

So, feeling slightly tipsy and eager to escape the noise, I left and returned to Captain's House.

It had developed into a lovely evening. The moon, full and bright, shone like the light from God's eye—seeing everything, caring about nothing. The balminess of the air, the freedom of the wind, the motion of the palm fronds made me feel like I was somewhat removed from this reality. As though life and time were moving forward and I was standing still. I could see and hear everything, but it was all moving faster than I was. I felt unfettered, independent, bound to no laws, no morality, no society.

The feeling was so exhilarating I decided to take a dip in the pool. Feel its sensuous embrace and cool detachment. I figured it would be empty, of people, and quiet out there. I could pretend that the entire backyard of the house was my private domain, in which I ruled and controlled everything. I didn't even bother to fetch a swimsuit. I'd get naked and be one with the lazy water.

But when I stepped out onto the deck I found Janis sitting on a lounge chair, alone, smoking a cigarette.

"Good evening," I said. "Sorry to intrude."

"Oh, it's all right. Actually, I could use some company."

"Where is everybody?"

"As far as the guests go, who knows? Aurelio's gone to the movies and Pearl is, well, angry with me."

I waited to see if she wanted to delve into this; tell me what was wrong. Or if she'd change the subject. But she was silent. I followed her example and listened to the sounds of the night—cicadas and the rustling of palms, the water sighing and chuckling.

"America sucks," she said, for no apparent reason.

"Huh?"

"America sucks."

"Oh?" I didn't have to wait long for an explanation. "That's what Pearl and I are fighting about."

"America?"

"Yeah."

"I see."

"She loves it, I hate it."

"How do you account for her love and your hate?"

She took a few moments to organize her thoughts. "In the last election I voted Democrat and she voted Republican."

"So?"

"Well, like, it was a real joke, y'know? No one voted for the candidates or the policies. You know what everyone voted for?"

"No," I said, "tell me."

"They voted for the commercials."

"What?"

"The television commercials. It's like—Anita Baker has the better records, but Whitney Houston has the best covers. You know?"

It didn't take long for her words to sink into the soft grayness of my cerebral cortex. And as soon as penetration was complete, an alarm sounded in my auditory canal. She was correct. I couldn't argue with her. In America, packaging is everything.

"What are you thinking about?" she asked.

I decided it was time to alter the course of the conversation.

"Janis," I said, "can you tell me what you did and what you saw last Thursday night?"

"What do you mean?"

"Tell me about your evening, from about eight until you went to sleep."

"Well, I probably started off watching television—but I'll have to check the *TV Guide* to see what I watched."

"If you started at eight, how long did you watch?"

"Probably until eleven."

"Then what?"

"I went to the kitchen to make a sandwich."

"Did you see anything unusual?"

"No. Nothing unusual. Let me see...I had a ham and

cheese sandwich and I ate it here, by the pool.

"Was anyone else around?"

"No. Why all the questions?"

"Because I want to find out what happened and why."

"Why?"

"Just my nature, I guess."

"Oh," she said, then stretched her thin arms with feline grace. She yawned, stood up. "Well, I think I'm about ready to go back inside and do battle with Pearl."

"Good luck."

"Thanks. 'Night."

I watched her lope back into the house. She closed the sliding glass door behind her. As soon as she was inside I stripped, piled my clothing on the deck and dove into the water. It was cool. I floated on my back with my eyes closed, not thinking, not feeling, just being. Not caring, worrying or scheming, just breathing. For a while I was free of my obsession. It was like a furlough from military duty. Instead of having to be spit-shined with a clean rifle and polished belt buckle, I was off-duty, away from the front, recuperating from shell shock. My brain was empty, my conscience on vacation, my ambition temporarily out of order.

It was miraculous, I suppose, that I was able to spend a few moments without fretting over Walter Burgess. But soon enough, other thoughts began to invade the peaceful territory of my mind. Like thoughts of Paul. I couldn't understand why he was being so hostile on the telephone. We'd been apart before and he hadn't acted so suspicious. Perhaps there was something happening that I didn't know about. Maybe our relationship was not as solid and secure as I'd imagined.

I was drifting around, eyes closed, legs and arms thrust out like the points of a star. I was a leaf floating on the surface of an Alpine lake. A snowflake whirling through the sky. A spinning mote in a shaft of morning sunlight.

My arm touched the side of the pool. I pushed myself back towards the center. And suddenly heard a loud splashing noise. I opened my eyes and lifted my head to see what was happening. Then, from out of a void, I felt hands pulling at me. Someone had a grip on my ankles. I was being pulled under. A kick to my stomach—even though its impact was diluted by the water—doubled me over. I gasped for breath as my head went under. Then I felt the hands, powerful hands, around my throat. My head was beneath the surface, my nostrils starting to fill. I kicked my legs out with all of my strength, trying to combat my attacker. Suddenly, strong fingers entangled my hair. I panicked. My head moved farther from the surface. My limbs were flailing about without connecting to anything. I couldn't breathe. My lungs felt like balloons stretched beyond the limit.

Then cool darkness crept into all my pores, spreading icy black ink through my veins, obscuring my consciousness, erasing my memory.

While I ceased to have any awareness of it, the world kept spinning and circling the sun, as oblivious to me as I was to it.

THIRTEEN

It was like those moments in a piece of music when all the instruments are quiet while the rhythm continues silently. Then all of the instruments come back in on a certain beat, creating a wall of sound that—after the tension-filled void—comes thundering back to realign the listener with the pulse. I was like a percussionist marking time, waiting to smash the cymbal. And smash it I did.

When I regained consciousness it was like the big crescendo at the end of a symphony. The world—in all of its sensuous detail—surrounded my being in a frenzy of eighth notes. I went from total silence to peak volume in a nanosecond.

Voices resonated in my ears. Whirling pinwheels of light stabbed at my retinas, I coughed up chlorinated water. In the living room, Janis, Pearl and Aurelio hovered like maiden aunts.

I was attempting to piece everything together, but at first, I was too confused. Eventually everything began to take on the glow of familiarity and I was able to grasp that someone had tried to drown me.

"If I hadn't come out to see if I left my cigarettes you'd have been a goner," said Janis.

"I don't know what to say except thank you," I wheezed.

"It was nothin'," she said. "Anyone would have done it."

Anyone except whoever was trying to kill me.

"Aurelio will help you to your room," said Pearl.

"I don't need any help," I said, trying to stand up. But I felt dizzy and sank back down. "Let me try again," I said,

107

and this time, rose slowly.

"Go with him," said Pearl.

I draped my arm around Aurelio's shoulders and we slowly made our way up the stairs and into my room.

I sat on the bed. Aurelio stood there staring at me. The clock said almost two.

"I'll go now," he said.

"I'd really appreciate it if you'd stay for a while," I said, still shaking.

"Okay, boss," he grinned and flung himself into the armchair. "Would you like some tea?"

"Yes," I said.

He dashed off to fetch some, returning a few minutes later with tea and little cakes on a silver tray. He set about pouring, stirring, serving and I couldn't decide if he was *Gaspard de la Nuit, The Sorcerer's Apprentice* or *The Afternoon of a Faun*. But his slim, delicate limbs, his olive oil skin, his coltish body language and innocent eyes made me want to reach out, enfold him like a cocoon, and drift away on a river of lemonade spiked with rum.

In those few moments I wanted him. Not to plunder topsy-turvy in a frenzy of sexual abandon. But just to hold him like a child. I think I felt that if I could comfort and soothe him, I might be comforted and soothed myself. The thought that someone had tried to kill me made me feel vulnerable, like a water balloon plummeting toward concrete. Maybe, sometimes, when a parent embraces a child to quell the youngster's tears, it is really the elder who benefits from the touch. If I could have thought of a way of clutching Aurelio to my chest—without him getting the wrong idea—I would have taken him beneath my blanket and rocked him in my arms until we both felt that everything was as good as it could get. But I gave no indication of this desire. I crossed my arms over my chest and spoke to Aurelio in a carefully, controlled, neutral tone of voice.

"How is it?" he asked.

I sipped some, Earl Grey, and told him it was fine.

"What happened?"

"I was swimming. I thought I was alone. And all of a sudden there was someone in the pool with me, dragging me under. I was struggling to breathe and then I blacked out.

That's all I know."

Aurelio looked at me with a strange expression on his face. That got my curiosity going. "Do you know anything about it?" I asked.

"No!" he said, like a scared jackrabbit. The vehemence of his denial made me doubt him.

"Is there something you're not telling me?"

"No!"

The gears in my brain started clicking. From out of nowhere I suddenly had a lot of questions to ask him.

"Aurelio. Last Thursday night. What did you do?"

He pretended to think about it for a second. "Nothing."

"Nothing?"

"Nothing."

"You must have done something. Did you watch television? Hang out with a friend?"

"I don't remember."

"Were you here at the house? Or somewhere else?"

I could tell he was thinking I was trying to trap him. He was correct. He screwed up his face as though he'd thrown his memory into overdrive. "At home. Here," he finally blurted.

"Did you see anything unusual?"

"No."

"Hear anything unusual?"

"No." He drained his teacup. "I must go now. I'll come back later for the tray."

He was out the door before I could say another word.

I was tired. Needed sleep. After making a mental note to question him again, I got ready for bed.

My muscles felt like overcooked asparagus; my brain like cold oatmeal. I needed sleep. Badly. The bed was quite comfortable but I couldn't relax. I wondered, should I contact the police? Tell them an attempt had been made on my life? But I realized they didn't care whether I lived or died. Not a particularly warm thought to ponder as you're trying to fall asleep.

But eventually I crossed the barrier into dreamland. The thing about dreams, though, is they can unexpectedly turn into nightmares.

I'm flying. Sensational. And not only can I become air-

109

borne at will, there is nothing to prevent me from flying through solid objects. Unlike Superman who must execute take-offs and landings where windows are situated, I am able to move through walls of concrete if I choose. Neat. But then, as I'm gliding out of an edifice and into the ionosphere, a cannonball slams into my chest and I fall to Earth, landing in the middle of a dark forest. Not very realistic. Like the set of *A Midsummer Night's Dream*. The next thing I know I'm tied to a plank, on a conveyor belt, heading toward a rotating sawmill blade. With needle-sharp spikes on it. I get closer and closer and as I do, I grow more terrified. I struggle mightily against the binding ropes. But I only succeed in abrading my wrists and ankles; the restraints will not give. Then my plank reaches the whirling steel. It's just like a cartoon scenario I've seen on television. My crotch moves closer, inch-by-inch to the buzzing, angry blade. Past my ankles, to my knees, my thighs coming together like the branches of a tree about to be pruned. But then, miraculously, just like in those cartoons, I awaken before anything organic is damaged.

There was a knocking at my door. I opened my bleary eyes. Realized it was only a dream. Nightmare. The clock said ten-thirty. More knocking.

"Who is it?" I yelled.

"It's Frank Fiore."

What could he possibly want?

I got up, went to the door, realized I was naked. "What is it?"

"Can I come in? It's important."

"Can it wait?"

"No, it can't."

"Okay," I said, trying not to sound too disappointed. I threw on a robe and admitted him. "I just woke up," I explained. He didn't apologize. "And I have to pee." He nodded. I went to the bathroom.

Splashed cold water on my face. It helped. Coffee would have been useful. The water felt so good. I turned on the shower. Doused myself under cold water. At first I got goose bumps. But they subsided. And I really woke up. Peed down the drain. Soaped myself from hair to toenails. Rinsed it all off. And toweled myself as I went back into the room.

Frank sat in the easy chair skimming my Anne Tyler. I got into my robe, slipped out of the towel and sat on the bed.

He plunged into his speech without offering a prologue. "I hear you're investigating Walter's death. Legalities aside, I have some information that may be valuable. Of course, there's a price for everything, my friend. No such thing as a free lunch! So, the reason why I came knocking so early is to make you an offer you can't refuse. You don't have much time to think about it because I'm going home tomorrow. So it's now or never. Or rather, sometime today or never. What do you think?"

He kept time with his left foot, a slightly martial beat, probably to the tune of the different drummer that battered the dried skins in his ear. I have to admit I was a bit flabbergasted. In the first place, what kind of information did he have? Second, what kind of bounty would I have to pay to get it?

"Well, Frank, this is a little early for me. Haven't even had any coffee yet. What's up?"

"One hears things, makes assumptions, adds two and two to get four."

"I see." He'd probably overheard something at breakfast. Most likely an exchange between Pearl, Janis and Aurelio. "And what kind of information are you peddling?"

"Someone told you a lie. I know the truth."

"I see." I almost laughed. Not only had one person told me one lie, but approximately ten people had told me approximately eight hundred lies. And as far as he knowing the truth goes, well, that was something I'd have to wait to find out about. "What kind of price, what coin of what realm are we talking about?"

With a completely deadpan expression he said, "Your ass."

Needless to point out, I was not expecting this. Did that mean that he wanted to kill me? Or fuck me? Or what? I didn't know what to say and figured if I didn't say anything, he'd be forced to elaborate.

Finally he did. "You're probably a bit shocked. But goddamnit! I came here to have a good time and so far I haven't even been laid once! And I've had my eye on your butt. And you need something. And I want something. Fair exchange? What do you say?"

Well, I had to admit that getting propositioned was certainly better than getting raped. I mean, he could have entered my room with a gun and forced me. At least I had a choice. And, though his face and personality were very unappetizing, he did have a nice body. Bulging thighs, generous basket, solid buns. And I wanted to get laid too. Hadn't had a dick up my ass in a long time. I missed the satisfaction. But I still needed a little persuading. "Not a very romantic proposition," I said, stalling.

"I already tried that on you and it didn't work. Now I have some bargaining power."

I weighed his offer in my mind. I couldn't know beforehand whether the information he had would be helpful. But it did occur to me that I might enjoy getting fucked by Frank if I didn't have to eat with him, dance with him, or spend time whispering sweet nothings and trying to discover the meaning of life. A fuck is a fuck.

"I accept your offer," I said, trying not to grin.

"I'll tell you what you want to know *after* you give me what I want."

I didn't argue. I'd go with it. Even if he reneged, even if his information was useless, I just might have as good a time as he would. I'm no fool.

"Fine. When and where?"

"What's wrong with right here and now?"

"Nothing," I said as nonchalantly as I could.

I took off my robe.

"Okay," he said, standing up, kicking off his sandals, removing his clothes. Good body. Hairy and hard.

We lay down side by side on the bed. "You lead," I said.

"Wait a second." He got up and walked to his pile of clothing. Reached for his shorts and pulled something from a pocket. I thought it was poppers. I was wrong. He tore open the packet, took out a condom and placed it on the night table. "I'm into safe sex," he said.

"Good. We'll need some lube." I got up, went to the bathroom and returned with some after-tanning lotion. With the scent of coconut oil.

Frank made a big production of greasing himself, getting hard, slipping the condom over his sizable cock.

"You want me on my back, stomach, or side?"

"Whichever you prefer."

A gentleman. I stretched out on my back, brought my knees up and threw my ankles into the air. I slid into the awaiting delivery mode. He eased himself in. It felt too tight for a second. Then, like a flood of opium balm washing me away. I lubed my palm and stroked myself. I felt him spurt deep within me. I came immediately thereafter. It only lasted a few moments. But they were the best moments of my entire stay in Key West.

It took him a few seconds to rejoin me on the plane of naked reality. His eyes looked like they'd seen God's diary.

Frank used the bathroom first. Then I entered and took another shower, hot. And we lolled on my bed like two high school girls gossiping about the captain of the football team.

"Your turn," I said, feeling in control now that he had to even things up.

"A bargain is a bargain," he said. "This morning just before breakfast I overheard a brief exchange between Pearl and Aurelio."

He paused dramatically.

"I'm listening," I said.

"They didn't know I could hear them. Aurelio told her that you'd asked him a lot of questions about the fatal night. And he told her that he lied to you."

"That's very interesting," I said.

"So? Who killed Walter?"

"I'm not sure yet," I said, "but I think I'm getting closer every minute."

"Who are the key suspects?"

"That would be telling," I said. "Everyone's a suspect until I'm certain of the culprit."

Frank's eyes narrowed and his cheeks flamed crimson. "Are you accusing *me?*"

"I'm accusing *everyone*. To tell you the truth, Frank, *I'm* the only person who I'm certain had nothing to do with it."

The expression on his face told me he was insulted, hurt, furious. He leaped off the bed, dressed, departed the room without another word and slammed the door.

I didn't let his anger get to me. Ordinarily I'd feel badly if I caused anyone any grief. But this murder stuff was serious business and I didn't care who I inconvenienced in the search for the truth.

But the truth would have to wait for a while. I was hungry. No, starving. Breakfast was over. I'd have to leave the house to get a proper meal.

So I dressed and left. It was almost noontime. I walked to Duval Street, on the shady side. Passed Simon and Griffith. Simon ignored me. Griffith nodded.

When I arrived at the Excelsior Cafe I sat down and looked at the menu. Just then, Regina passed by. She saw me and waved. Then she came in and asked if she could join me.

"Sure," I said.

She didn't look very well. Her hair was unkempt and her eyes looked puffy.

FOURTEEN

"You look tired," I said, "are you all right?"

Regina nodded. "I'm fine. Just a little upset. I think I'm beginning to feel the impact now. Right after I found out he was dead I couldn't express anything because it would have given me away. To Joyce. So I just made myself feel numb. But now she knows. He's gone. Nothing really matters. And all of this feeling is overwhelming me."

I looked at her and felt badly for her. My heart wanted to reach out and comfort her. It must be horrible to love someone with whom you've been having a secret affair. When it's over you can expect no consolation without revealing the secret. And if your lover has died violently, that can only add to your feeling of despair. And, if, in addition to that, your lover was murdered and you are one of the prime suspects, it must be something like hell—raw pain layered on excruciating hurt to the degree of infinity.

Regina ordered a bacon cheeseburger, I a Spanish omelette. We both craved coffee.

"How much longer will you be around?" I asked her.

"Another day or two. I've had enough. Got to get home."

I had to confront her with unpleasant questions, so I thought I'd ease into it with some lubricating words. "I really enjoyed hearing what you had to say the other night about symphonies and scary movies."

She brightened. "Outside of teenagers not many people think about music much anymore."

"Sure seems that way," I said, preparing for the big question. "Regina, about Walter's murder—"

"It was a suicide. And yes, I was there."

"What were you doing there?"

"Telling Walter that Joyce and I were in town."

"But he already knew."

"Right, but we didn't know that he knew at that point," she said. "It was late at night and Joyce had already fallen asleep. I was just tossing and turning. If I called I would have woken her up. So what I did was get dressed, walk to the house and ring the bell. A nice man—I think his name was Edward—let me in and showed me to Walter's room. I knocked on the door and then Walter and I went down to the pool to talk. And then we swam for a while. Then I left."

"You rang the bell?"

"Yes."

"What time was this?"

"Oh, sometime around midnight. I'm not absolutely sure."

"I see." If she was telling the truth then Aurelio and Janis were lying. No one ever rings the bell that late. And they'd both claimed that nothing unusual had happened that night. I didn't want Regina to know that I'd uncovered this discrepancy so I changed the subject. "Would you give me your home address and number?"

"Of course," she said, and wrote the information on the back of a store receipt.

We talked a bit more about how lovely Key West is. Then she told me about some of her favorite film scores. After splitting the bill and departing, she kissed me on the cheek and went back to her hotel.

I wanted to spend some time in the pool, and lolling in the sun. Needed time to think about how to proceed. Whom to confront, in what order, and what to ask. So I went back to the house all set to change into my Speedos, grab my sunscreen and Anne Tyler, then get lazy by the pool.

But as soon as I walked through the front door Edward came into the hall from the living room. "Ah, there you are," he said, "do you have time for a brief chat?"

"Of course."

"My room?"

"Lead the way," I said.

His room gave me a shiver. I took one look at the chifforobe and was reminded of the dangerous game I was playing. Had

Simon and I been discovered in Edward's room, who knows what the consequences might have been?

"Beer, soda, vodka, orange juice?" he asked after closing the door.

I sat on the sofa. "Whatever you're having."

"Never too early for a screwdriver," he said.

I watched him mix the drinks. Sexy, handsome, intelligent, successful. Not bad. He came over beside me. The cocktail was far too strong for my constitution.

"Word is out," he said. "I understand you're making a federal case of Walter Burgess's death."

I could tell right away he was trying to intimidate me. But I didn't fall for it—I immediately attacked and put him on the defensive. "I have it on the best authority that the name, address and telephone number of Walter Burgess are in your directory. And you told me you'd never met him."

Edward's face displayed several color schemes before settling on a shiny indigo. "How...who told you?" he sputtered.

"A little birdy."

He harumphed and gulped the rest of his drink in one quick motion. I didn't dare tell him how I'd found out.

"So what of it? I've got lots of names in my book. Some of them are people who handed me a business card and then I transferred the information and never used it. I've had that directory for years. Maybe I met him ten years ago and forgot about it. Okay?"

He leaped to his feet and made himself another drink. His story was plausible. Certainly, I too have many names, addresses and numbers I've never made use of. Still. This was too much of a coincidence. I tried to catch him off guard. "Who told you about the federal case I'm supposed to be making?"

"Skip. He thinks you think he's the murderer."

"Maybe I do."

"Really?"

"Or maybe I think it's you," I said, cool as sorbet.

"Me? But I had no motive. I never even met the guy."

"But you do have his address."

Edward looked helpless. Like he might cry any second. I left before things could get any more bathetic. Went to my room and plopped on the bed. I felt a little strange. Like I

117

was speeding. My mind was going so fast I couldn't reach out and grab anything. It was like my brain was a video-cassette on fast forward and I couldn't turn the damn machine off.

What was I doing? Making reckless accusations, lying, violating peoples' privacy, being bothersome, obnoxious, unethical and completely unlike my usual self. In seeking the truth I'd become a deceiver. Attempting to codify a reality, I'd created too many illusions. I was certainly as immoral and reprehensible as whoever it was who had destroyed Walter. And I'd thrown my entire existence into a lopsided dance routine in pursuit of something which I knew nothing about. I couldn't for the life of me figure out why I'd played this tune or how I'd chanced upon the choreography.

But the shard in my brain that had the most salient points, the sharpest edges, was the one that screamed to me how wrong I was in all of my assumptions. All along I'd been certain that the tragedy had been the work of a lone assailant. A single crazed individual. What had been eluding me was the obvious teamwork which must have gone into this act. It was unavoidable. I had to admit to myself that I was dealing with a conspiracy. Beneath the casual relations of all the people I'd met—Skip, Frank, Edward, Pearl, Janis, Aurelio, Regina, Joyce—there had to be some connecting threads, some kind of arrangement. They'd plotted and planned and made up stories and covered for each other, all in an effort to keep me from the truth. And I was so inept, so stupid, so willing to lap up their lies. They'd had me spinning along a figure-eight of falsity and I'd been totally unaware.

It had to be about drugs. Nothing else could be lucrative enough to involve so many people. Probably boats from Bolivia with mountains of cocaine. There was some kind of network that they were all involved in, or some of them, and one of them had cheated the others. Walter was probably the swindler and the rest had conspired to exact their revenge.

And just as soon as I realized that I was battling a corporation and not an individual, an ugly epiphany smacked me across the face. They had me! I was trapped! Edward and Frank had tried to pump me to see just how much of a threat I was to them. By now, they'd told everyone else. If I should attempt to leave the room, I'd probably never make it to the front door. They'd drown me. Or slit my throat and dismember me. If they were clever about it, they could probably carry off my demise with as much ease and lack of incriminating evidence as they had Walter's.

It seemed so simple all of a sudden. It was like I'd been tossing the pieces of a puzzle into the air and—just through sheer luck and persistence—for once they'd fallen into place. As soon as I realized that I was battling a well-organized team, everything became so obvious. The way they'd accused each other of lying. It had worked! They'd foiled me! I might as well have been trying to perform brain surgery wearing a blindfold and boxing gloves.

But now, I had two choices. Wait for them to silence me forever or try to save myself. Somehow. My first thought was to call Paul. Even if he was angry with me, I knew he'd help me out if I was in serious trouble. I hoped.

It occurred to me that someone could be listening right outside my door. Aurelio was a quiet little spy. I picked up the telephone and dialed as quietly as I could. When the phone began to ring, to my ears it sounded like the clanging of Big Ben. I had to force myself to realize that nobody else could hear it. It rang three times. An eternity. Then the machine picked up. Shitfuck. Paul wasn't home. After the beep I whispered, "Paul, you've got to help me...I'm trapped in the guest house in Key West...they're going to kill me...you've got to call the local cops and ask for Sergeant Simon...tell him I'm in danger and I'm at the house." I hung up the receiver as quietly as I could.

My heart had begun to respond to my racing brain. Its four chambers and one aorta slammed faster and harder. Sweat ran down my forehead and back. I felt like I couldn't breathe, that my ribcage would shatter. For a brief moment I saw myself splattered at the bottom of an empty black marble pool.

I tried deep breathing. I had to slow myself down so I could think. Stop the pain and end the madness. I tried breathing from the diaphragm, like a basso profundo. As slowly as I could, I pulled all the air I could get down deep into my lungs. I held it there. Then let it out slowly. Again. It seemed to help a little.

I was huddled on my bed against the headboard in the dark. Beyond my door were people who wanted to see me dead. The really scary part was that they could easily end my life and successfully conceal it. No one would ever know. They'd make up alibis for one another, tell any story they had to in order to protect themselves from prosecution.

I was already as good as gone.

And then a zigzag of lightning darted through my mind. Paul might not get my message in time. And if he did, he might not take it seriously.

I had one more option. To call the police myself. I found the number and began to dial. Relief flooded my consciousness. But when the phone rang twice and the officer answered, I slammed the receiver down. How could I be so stupid? The police were in on it! That's why they'd dropped the investigation. That's why Simon humored me when I wanted to get into Edward's room! I immediately called Paul and left a message canceling the previous one.

I realized there was no hope. Eventually I'd have to leave my room. And the gang of murderers waiting for me out there would make damn sure I'd never be heard from again.

But they might not wait until I found the courage or stupidity to leave. They might just come for me. And the lock would be of no use because Pearl and Aurelio had keys.

I bounced off the bed and started rearranging the furniture. First I pushed the armchair across the room and propped it against the door, then jammed the bed against the chair.

I was safe.

Unless someone decided to shatter the windows and come in from the veranda.

I began to cry. Big heaving sobs to accompany the dripping tears. I felt helpless. Vulnerable. I was certain that I'd never hear another concert, never see another New York sidewalk, never again taste male flesh.

I don't know how long I sat there weeping. But I recall that my eyes were very red and sore. I had achy muscles in my chest and back. My brain felt like it had been stir-fried and I was weary to the marrow.

Eventually I must have caught a glimpse of sanity. I

began to restore my room to its former state. The bed and chair were returned to their original positions.

I tried, in a cool, rational manner, to regain a sense of stability, or purpose. And eventually realized I'd be better off making an offensive move instead of waiting to be attacked. I attempted to formulate a plan.

But it was too late. I heard a knock at my door. And immediately figured I'd reached the end. I'd been caught. There was no place to go. I'd been butting into other peoples' private affairs and I was about to pay the exorbitant bill.

I didn't even ask who it was. Just opened the door in defeat.

Skip rushed into the room. By the light from the hall I could see blood on his arms and face. He looked at me with terror in his eyes. "Quick! Lock the door!" he screamed. "She's trying to kill me!"

"Who?" I asked, panicked, my heart slamming again, my brain on fire.

"Quick!" he shouted and hurled himself against the door. His shirt was slashed. There were gashes on his forearms with blood streaming. Red smears on his jeans.

I rushed to the door. He was fumbling with the lock. But his fingers, slippery with blood, couldn't get a grip. I pushed him away. "I'll do it," I said. "We've got to take care of your wounds."

He looked down at his arms. Lifted them. His eyes stared in disbelief.

I tried to grasp the bolt, but it was too slicked with blood. I tore off my shirt to dry it so I could get some traction. Then, suddenly, the knob turned from the other side and the door flung open. Regina rushed into the room. She had a knife, dripping, and a demented look in her eyes. She stared at Skip then at me, as if trying to decide who she should kill first.

I had no idea what was happening. I instinctively backed away from her and found myself with my back to the wall. Skip gasped for breath and stood in a crouch, ready to move in any direction. Regina sliced the air with the knife and moved toward him. I was frozen like a marble statue.

Then Pearl flew into the room. She came up behind Regina and hit the back of her neck with a martial arts chop.

121

As Regina crumpled to the floor the knife dropped from her hand. Pearl rushed to Skip and grabbed his arms. "This is bad," she said, leading him into the bathroom. As the light came on, Officers Griffith and Simon entered the room. They looked at me, then at Regina, sprawled on the floor. I stood still, pressed against the wall, trying to catch my breath, and watched as they took Regina away. And when Skip emerged from the bathroom with towels tied around his forearms and Pearl led him out, I curled on my bed. Completely confused and worn out. Too weak to do anything except float like a microorganism in a ten-foot wave, until dashed on the rocky shore, you wait in a dark tidepool, inert and lifeless until another wave picks you up, or until the sun dries you out and the wind blows you away.

I must have slept for at least twelve hours.

FIFTEEN

I was as groggy as a drunk or as dazed as a new-born babe when I awoke. There were blood stains on the floor and bedspread, like some kind of weird Rorschach. Looking at them I could detect images of evil, despair, death.

I recalled Skip's entrance, Regina's follow-up, Pearl's daring rescue, the inevitable Keystone Cops. But I could make no sense of it. I felt like I was looking through a kaleidoscope but there was not enough light to determine the actual colors or shapes of what appeared to be shapeless gray debris.

Showering helped. A lot. But I still felt fog-bound as I dressed and descended the stairs in search of coffee. The house was quiet as I walked to the back.

On the pool deck the sun shone warm and bright. There were people in the pool whom I didn't recognize. New guests, I surmised. After greeting them, I poured myself some coffee and began to sip it. Minutes later I felt somewhat restored. My sight was clear. My thoughts flowing. I felt no pressure or strain. Weightless as though in a space capsule.

Another cup. Then Pearl emerged from the house. Her eyes looked red and she had a bandanna around her hair.

"Come with me," she said, and led me into her room.

It was completely different from the rest of the house. Like a life-size doll house: lace doilies, embroidery, small figurines everywhere. In shades of coral, lime, black, white and gray. It was colorful, but subdued. Feminine and child-like with a glaze of nostalgia. Everything looked so delicate and fragile. I was afraid that a careless gesture or loud utterance might shatter something.

Janis sat on a divan, filing her nails. She nodded in my direction, then went into another room and closed the door behind herself.

"I have a few things to say," said Pearl, indicating that we should sit. "I'm not sure where to begin, so I'll start with my grandfather."

I nodded.

She told me about his rum-running days, as told to her by her mother. When the Caribbean was caught between the death of buccaneering and the birth of modern sea trade. How all of this played a part in the development of the tiny island at the southernmost tip of Florida.

"...And when he finally retired, he settled here and built this house. But, you know, people never knew how he died. Except for our family, of course. We kept it a secret. Because it was considered sinful to take your own life. But he was dying of some disease or other—I never knew for certain. And he was in so much pain. When I was a girl I cried every time Mama told me about it. When the pain became too much for him, he decided to end his life. So he went out to the backyard, stuck a gun in his mouth and pulled the trigger...he was found exactly in the same spot as we found poor Walter. Of course, there was no pool back in those days. But when I came out here and saw that body in the bottom of the pool, it did something to me. I guess you might say I felt that this death had to be hushed up the same way as my grandfather's. I thought, if people knew a murder took place here, they'd never want to come and be guests. I apologize for avoiding your questions and flying off the handle and all. I admit, I didn't cope with it well at all. But it wasn't because I wanted to obstruct justice or anything. I just wanted to protect my business like my family tried to protect our reputation."

That certainly explained why Pearl had been so uncooperative. But it told me nothing about Walter's death.

"I understand," I said. "For a moment I thought you had to be in on it because of the way you seemed to deal with it. But I understand now. Really."

"So, we're still friends, right?"

"Right," I said. "But Pearl, I'm still confused about a lot of stuff. Like last night. What happened? Who called the police? How did you know to come to my room when you did?"

"Well, it was obvious something was amiss. For one thing, you seemed to be acting pretty strangely for the last few days..."

I blushed.

"...and then last night I was helping Aurelio and Janis do some touching up in the hallway. He did a great job but there were a few spots that needed work. Anyway, it must have been about sometime after ten. The door opened and Skip came in, bleeding, and he just ran up the stairs. I thought that was pretty odd! Then, just a minute later, this lady came in—and she had a key! I don't know where she got it from. But she had a key to my house! And she ran upstairs like she owned the place! So the first thing I did was call the police. Then I went upstairs and found her trying to slice and dice you guys. Once the police arrived, I took Skip to the hospital."

"How is he?"

"All right. A bit spooked more than anything, I'd say. He wants to talk to you when he comes back. Which should be sometime today."

"That's good," I said.

We talked for a few more minutes. She told me about some new marketing plans she had in mind. A few renovations that she figured would help to attract more customers. Among other things, I told her that I was homesick and anxious to leave.

When I got back to my room I picked up the telephone receiver and made two calls: first, to the airline. I booked a flight back to New York for the following morning. Then, to Paul. He wasn't home. I left a message telling him my time of arrival. When I heard his voice on tape it made me realize how much I missed him. Suddenly, the time between now and when my plane was to depart seemed like a protracted eternity.

Hunger pangs began to chomp at my stomach lining. I went to Duval Street and ate a huge meal at one of those family restaurants where the menu is like a billboard and they serve everything from scrambled eggs to coq au vin. The food wasn't exquisitely prepared, but it was filling. I had a shrimp cocktail, mushroom barley soup, tossed salad, stuffed porkchops, chocolate cake and felt like a blimp as I trudged back to the house. To sit in the sun. To swim. To read. To relax.

But when I walked through the door, Skip was waiting for me. Both his arms were bandaged from the wrists to the elbows. He had a bruise on his forehead and a Band-Aid on his cheek. "If you don't mind," he said, "I'd like to speak to you in my room."

"I don't mind," I said and we walked, slowly, up the stairs.

He offered me a beer but I was too stuffed. He sipped from a can. "I don't know where to start," he said.

"Why did you and Walter take separate rooms?"

"In case he wanted to pretend he didn't know me."

"How long did you work for him?"

"About four years. There were others before me."

"Where did Regina get a key from?"

"From Walter. As soon as she got down here he had one made for her so she could slip away from Joyce, come to the house and have sex with him."

"So, it must have been Regina who pushed me in the pool and tried to drown me."

Skip's face flushed with embarrassment. "Wrong. It was me."

"You?"

"Yes. Let me explain. Regina persuaded me that you were going to pin the rap on me, and she convinced me to try to scare you away. Really, I never wanted to harm you. Just frighten you a little."

"It worked. I was frightened. But why did Regina try to kill you last night? What was that all about?"

"After the police took all of Walter's stuff away, I had next to nothing. No way to get back home. So I went to Regina and asked her if she'd spot me some money. She said no. So I started doing a little freelance hustling to try to raise the bucks. You see, all along Walter was telling her I was straight and just pretending. But the thing was, I wasn't honest with either of them. I needed the job with Walter and he was afraid that if he hired a real gay guy he might be seduced. He wanted a straight guy to pretend. So I pretended I was straight for Walter's sake and when we were around gay clients, we acted like a couple. Anyway, I ran into Regina last night and she made a snide remark about me going back home and I told her I'd already earned the bread. I guess she always suspected I was gay but last night she realized for sure that I am and I guess she thought that all this time Walter was fooling around with guys and me in particular and she just got into a rage. All of a sudden she whips this knife out from her purse and starts ripping me up." He looked down at his bandaged arms, then up at me. Like a whipped kitten. I felt a flood of compassion for him.

"It was then that I realized that she must have killed him, which I never suspected before, so I ran to tell you so you would stop thinking it was me. But she followed me. Literally running down the street with a bloody knife. It was too weird. She must really be nuts. Something I always suspected. But last night was, whew! Walter too. Both of them. Totally nuts. I'm glad this is all over. As soon as I get these bandages off I'm going home. Look for a new line of work."

"One more thing. That stuff about getting drugged? Remember when you claimed that someone had spiked your drink?"

"I made that up," he said, embarrassed.

"Did Walter know Edward Mallinson? Were they friends?"

"Not that I know of."

"I think that ties up all my loose ends," I said.

"Your persistence is amazing," said Skip.

"Yeah, that's what my lover always says after we have sex," I quipped.

Skip laughed as I hoped he would. He had a great smile. The tension was broken. The parting would be less difficult. We exchanged phone numbers and promised to get together sometime in New York. He kissed my cheek and I left his room.

I figured I'd better pack. Rather than leave it for the last thing in the morning. There wasn't a whole lot. Mainly a week's worth of dirty laundry. I'd be taking more memories than objects. I left out my toilet articles and clothing to travel in.

127

Then I sat down to finish my Anne Tyler.

But having read only a handful of pages, I heard a knock on my door.

Aurelio.

He looked sad. I invited him in. He accepted a Coke. I popped the tops of two cans. We went out onto the veranda and sat on the white wicker chairs.

"You're leaving," he said.

"Yes. It's all over for me."

"Pretty wicked shit," he mumbled.

I nodded. "Now that I know Regina did it and how she did it I feel like I can finally relax."

He looked at me gravely with his intense eyes and said, "It's not like everyone thinks."

I looked at him expectantly.

"I can trust you," he said, hesitated, then started speaking, maintaining a tight hold on his voice and language. "I don't have my green card yet. I didn't tell anyone anything because if I get into trouble they'll send me back to Uruguay."

"Go on," I urged.

"I saw the whole thing. I was hiding."

"Hiding? Where?"

"Underneath a lounge chair."

"Why?"

"Because I was out by the pool smoking a joint. If Pearl knew I smoked a joint..." he drew his finger across this throat. "And then they came out to swim."

"Who?"

"Walter and Regina. But they started arguing and she said she had to go to the bathroom."

"What were they arguing about?"

"He said he found out she was blackmailing him. He said she was using someone else to get money from him. He said they had to stop being together and she said she'd go crazy without him. So Walter waited until she went into the house to go to the bathroom and then he opened the valve to empty the pool. The water started to drain. When she came out she walked to the deep end of the pool and asked him why it was getting empty. He went over beside her and said it was emptied automatically every night. They argued some more.

128

He tried to push her in, they struggled, and she pushed him in."

I was astonished. "You mean, he was trying to kill her and she was trying to kill him?"

He nodded vehemently. "He was afraid of anything that might mess up his business. She was afraid of losing him. I said nothing because I am illegal." A tear crept down his cheek. "And that's not all."

"There's more?"

He nodded. "It was me who took the notebook from your room."

"You? Why?"

"Because I thought you wrote it. I wanted to be your friend. I thought if I read your book we could talk about it. But then when I read it I knew it belonged to someone else."

"So you returned it."

"Yes."

I was touched that he'd wanted to be my friend. "When we first met," I confided, "I thought all you wanted was sex."

"That too," he grinned.

"And to be paid for it," I added.

He jumped up, indignant. "Never will I take or give money for sex."

"Same here," I said.

He sat.

"I'm sorry if I offended you," I said.

"I'm sorry too."

He was adorable. But not the big, strapping hulk I wanted to maul me into a frenzy. Too slim. Too young. Legalities aside, I'm just not into kids. I like mature, experienced guys. But I didn't want Aurelio to think I was age-ist. When he would be old enough for me, I'd be too old for him. It was hopeless. I hoped he'd let it drop.

We finished our Cokes. I told him that I had to complete my packing. We embraced and he left.

I continued reading. Eventually my eyes grew weary. I looked at the clock. Almost ten o'clock. Too early to go to sleep. I thought I'd take one last trip to Duval Street to visit Woody's and Streets.

But I never made it.

Halfway there, I was crossing an intersection when Simon

stepped from a shadow. He intercepted me. We walked to the same alley where we'd met previously.

Most of the allure was gone. He still looked great. But my desire had wilted. I supposed he wanted another mouth-to-dick resuscitation. But I wasn't interested.

"I'm leaving tomorrow morning," I said. "If this thing should ever come to trial, I'll be back to testify. You know, there's an eyewitness."

"Oh, really?" he said, skeptical.

"Yes. Really."

"Who?"

"I'll only reveal that when forced to under oath."

"I see," he said. And licked his lips. I wished I could see into his mind. Inscrutable.

"Did you have something you wanted to discuss with me?" I asked. "I mean, why are we standing here in this alley, aside from the fact that you don't want to be seen with me?"

I could tell my words stung him like cold water on a January morning. Good, I said to myself.

"It's not that I don't want to be seen with you," he protested under his breath, "it's just that I can't deal with all the hassles. And I'd be risking my job."

"Good night," I said and turned to exit the alley.

"No, wait," he said and placed his hands on my shoulders. He turned me around to face him.

Then he knelt, unzipped my jeans and took me into his mouth.

He'd obviously had some experience with his lips and tongue. I loved the attention. I felt like a saxophone player in front of a big crowd, the band really swinging hot, and I'm waiting to take my solo. The tension keeps building as the band moves through the verse, chorus, bridge, and then with the loud crash of a cymbal, I spurted out a riff of high notes that soared like flaming arrows into the dark, velvety night sky.

Simon rose from the gravel, licking his lips. He kissed me on the cheek and disappeared into the shadows.

I zipped up. Headed back to Captain's House. I'd need some sleep before leaving. The trip would be an ordeal. Airport, flight, airport, flight, bad food, obnoxious passengers, New York traffic. And I'd have to smooth everything over with Paul. Lie to him about Simon. Not to mention the big shots at work. I'd have to lie and tell them that I'd almost drowned and went into shock and the doctor advised me to wait a few days before traveling. I'd probably have to write a stupid travel article whether I wanted to or not.

But I felt I could deal with anything. After all that I'd been through, everything would seem easy. This is what I told myself, walking through the warm, steamy air of Key West on my way back to Captain's House.